Maverick Rising

A Wicked Rogues Prequel

E.F. Rose

Maverick Rising
A Wicked Rogues Prequel, Book 0.5

Written by E.F. Rose
www.facebook.com/DarkestRose13

Copyright © 2023 by E.F. Rose

ISBN: 979-8-9852112-9-0

Edited by: Kim Young of Kim's Fiction Proofreading & Editing Services

Warning:

Intended for mature audiences only (18+). This book contains some naughty language, sexual content, and violence.

Maverick

I've been part of the Wicked Rogues MC for as long as I can remember. Giving my all to the club I love, even as I watch our President slowly tear it apart from the inside out. Now, brothers have started disappearing, and deals that had been in place for years are suddenly changing. Something needs to be done, and everyone's looking at me to make a move. I'm too old for this, but I'll do what I can. I owe my brothers that much. But the timing sucks. I hadn't planned on meeting a woman I've secretly longed for my whole life. Everything seems to be coming to a head sooner than we had planned, but I refuse to give up on my brothers...or my girl.

Jenny

I grew up in a life people are curious about. My dad is President of a motorcycle club called the Dead Man's Curse, and my brother is a member, so you can say it's in my blood. I've never known anything else. While the men in my life try to shield me from the darker side of things, I see the distress in their eyes, hear the anger in their voices. It doesn't help that one of the men they discuss, one they hope will fix everything they've been dealing with, is a man who piques my curiosity. But once I finally lay eyes on him, I know he's the one for me. My soulmate. Unfortunately, things are becoming dangerous. Once the dust settles, I just hope he comes for me. I know I'll wait for him.

This is a story of a man yearning for the safety he once knew, as well as the love of a woman he's always desired.

Welcome to the Wicked Rogues...

**** Maverick Rising was originally published in the Wrong Side of the Tracks anthology. There's been no changes made xx

"The dangers of life are infinite, and among
them is safety."

~ Goethe

Chapter 1
Maverick

March 19, 1990
Wicked Rogues' clubhouse
Shady Hills, California

The crack of metal hitting metal echoes through the gym. I haven't been in here long, but I already know this isn't having the desired effect. Basically, to take my mind off the meeting later tonight. As lucrative as our little side job is, my nerves are always shot the day of.

Especially lately.

I joined the Wicked Rogues motorcycle club the day I turned eighteen. This club is my life, my family, and I've spent the last twenty-two years devoting myself to it. The past few years, though, have been rough. Both personally and in the club.

Just thinking about it brings up images of the last time I saw my sister, Traci. It hurts, my stomach churning. She wasn't the person I remembered, loved. The drugs changed her, both physically and mentally, until she was someone I didn't recognize anymore.

I hadn't planned on getting into an argument when I pulled up to the house. But given the state of her when she opened the door...disheveled, pale, dark circles under her eyes, hair a mess, spitting a snarky comment as soon as she saw me...I should have known this was a bad idea.

I just wanted to help her. Beg her to go to rehab and get away from the sorry pieces of shit she clung to. But the conversation quickly turned heated. Words were said that couldn't be taken back. The sound of the door slamming in my face reverberated in the air.

That was almost two years ago. I looked for her, but it was like she disappeared. The feeling of guilt and pain clung to me every second of every day. I knew I had done everything I could, but it didn't make it any easier.

Around the same time, the club's president, Fat Mike, decided he wanted to change up how we did things.

Thinking about our President made my eyes twitch. Whereas some members of the club got their road names for their looks, others, like Fat Mike, got his for his actions. He's a gluttonous pig, period. With everything in life. Be it food, money, girls, alcohol. He can never get enough, and it's starting to catch up with him. His protruding gut, thinning, greasy hair, oily skin, "shit don't stink" attitude... However, his radical choices and increased agitation are the big signs his lifestyle had changed him. Which then changed the club.

Individuals we once had a decent relationship with wanted nothing to do with us, and Fat Mike began making deals with people I wouldn't trust to clean up after my dog. To make matters worse, several brothers ended up in the hospital, got locked up, or just vanished without a trace.

In fact, as far as I could tell, the only ones doing well during these last few years were Fat Mike and his inner circle.

Inner circle... Ha! It isn't even made up of club officers like it should be. It's just guys who kiss his ass and have the same viewpoint. I thought a few of them were good guys, but after recent events, I've started to question their loyalty to the club.

Even now, as I finish off my third set with the weights, I notice a few whispering amongst themselves, casting glances at me and the other brothers in the gym. One of the guys, Skeeter, keeps sneering when he thinks I'm not looking. I've never trusted that piece of shit, so it doesn't surprise me he's in Fat Mike's pocket.

Shaking my head, I do the last few reps when someone's pager chimes. I lower the weights back onto the rack as Skeeter pulls his pager from his pocket and looks at the screen, grinning.

I can't hear what he says to the guys around him as they begin to pack up their stuff, looking smug. As they walk past me, each one avoids making eye contact. Except Skeeter.

"Maverick," he sneers, his yellow teeth flashing behind chapped lips.

"Skeeter," I respond, nodding.

He scoffs, not stopping, I keep my eyes on them as they leave the room.

Blowing out a breath, I make eye contact

with the four brothers in the gym, receiving a mixture of raised eyebrows and shrugs, before walking toward the bench to grab my towel and water bottle. The door abruptly flies open. I glance up sharply, half expecting Skeeter to come walking back in.

Instead, Smoke strides in. His grey eyes flash as he makes his way toward me. I down my water as he stops by the bench. His analytical gaze scans the room before landing back on me.

"I saw Skeeter and the 'sheep' heading out." His glare deepens. "Heard Fat Mike was calling some sort of meeting."

I narrow my eyes. "The fuck? So *that* was the page."

"What page?"

"Right before they left, Skeeter got a page. Made them head out pretty damn quick."

Stuffing the end of my towel into my back pocket, I begin to head out, Smoke falling into step beside me. "How did you hear about his meeting?"

"Poot," he says.

E.F. Rose

I nod, understanding. Besides being the gassiest man around, Poot is also a big mouth. The guy can't keep a secret to save his soul.

"I'm surprised they told him."

"Me, too. Honestly, he probably just overheard the guys talking and took that as being included in the conversation."

"Probably," I sigh, heading up the stairs toward my room. Everyone has a room in the clubhouse, even if you live somewhere else.

Unlocking the door, I walk in, Smoke following and closing the door. "So, do we know what this meeting is about?" I ask.

"No fucking idea. But judging by their giddy expressions, it can't be anything good." Smoke blows out a breath, spinning my desk chair around and sitting, crossing his arms over the back. "I'm worried, Maverick."

"You're not alone," I respond, sitting on the edge of my bed.

Smoke nods as we both fall into a contemplative silence.

I am so tired of worrying over everything

lately. It started slowly. Just a few mishaps. Cops showing up randomly. Bikes having issues on runs. I really hadn't noticed anything at first, but it gradually began to add up until we all questioned everything. And I think we've all come to the same conclusion. Nothing over the past few years has been an accident. More like Fat Mike "cleaning house".

"Have you seen Dog lately?" Smoke suddenly asks.

I snap my eyes to his, slowly shaking my head and frowning. "Shit. I haven't seen him in days. Last time I did, he was pissed about something Fat Mike had said. I told him to just chill about it, lift weights if he needed to, but he told me he couldn't let it go.

"Fuck, Smoke. What the hell is going on?" I growl.

"I don't know, but he isn't the first one to go missing."

Nodding, I glance around the room. I really hoped the guys who had disappeared had just decided to leave the club life. The only other possibility made my chest tighten with rage.

"It can't keep going like this, Maverick. Are we all going to eventually disappear?"

I know Smoke is right. Something needs to be done, and soon, but I'm just not sure what. Damn, days like this exhaust me.

Smoke narrows his hard gaze at me. I frown. "What?"

"You know what," he growls

"No, I don't," I bite back, even though I have a pretty good idea.

"We're all waiting for you to decide."

"On what?"

He throws up his hands. "On what to do about the current situation."

Smoke closes his eyes and blows out a breath, then levels his gaze on me again. "Look, Maverick. I know I haven't been around as long as most of the guys, but I see the way they respond to you. The way they look to you when there's trouble, come to you when they need support. If you decide to make a move, to try and end this hell, I know the club will back you." He shrugs. "Sure, Fat Mike may have a small group at his bidding, but there are more who will follow you."

"I'm way too old for this shit, Smoke."

Being forty, I know I'm not ancient, but I'm not a spring chicken, either. Forcefully taking over a motorcycle club is a young man's game.

Have I mentioned I'm tired?

"Shut up. You're not *that* old," Smoke smirks, expression quickly sobering once again.

"Listen, I hate putting this on you, Maverick, and I'd happily go another route if we had one. But I'm afraid Fat Mike is going to burn this club to the ground if we don't do something soon."

And there it is. The crux of the situation. I know it. He knows it. Hell, the whole club knows it.

I blow out a breath and nod. "Okay. I'll call a meeting tomorrow with those we know are sick of things. Let's see where everyone else's head is before we make any big decisions."

Smoke stands, pushing the chair back under the desk.

"I don't need to tell you we can't have this getting around the clubhouse, Smoke. Don't imagine Fat Mike will appreciate us having a meeting without him."

"True. I'll head over to Dodger's house and let him know what's going on. We'll be back in time for the run tonight."

"Sounds good. Figure if we leave by five, we'll get to the warehouse on time."

Smoke nods before leaving the room, closing the door behind him.

Now that the decision has been made, my mind begins to spin with possibilities. With all the things that could go right...and wrong.

One thing I know for certain. This isn't a situation to rush into. I just hope everyone else agrees with that because, unfortunately, this could turn into a bloodbath really quickly.

Chapter 2
Jenny

Dead Man's Curse's clubhouse
Prodigy, California

"Where are you going?"

Turning, I spot Bev walking toward me. The wife of my dad's VP, Tread, she's my mother's closest friend...as well as a busybody. The fact I am thirty-seven doesn't matter. In her eyes, I'm still that child she played dress up with when she babysat me.

Don't get me wrong. I love the woman. But I just wish she'd stay out of my business. Like now. It's not like I'm even doing anything. Just heading to my dad's office to say goodbye before going home. But because of her tone, as well as the raised eyebrow, I feel like I got caught with my hand in the cookie jar.

"Hi, Aunt Bev."

"Hello, child. What are you up to today? You working at the shelter?"

Clearview is a shelter, a safe place for people who have been the victim of abuse. I started volunteering when I was in high school. I'd sit with some of the kids, watching movies or reading, and help around the shelter with any cleaning or shopping that needed to be done. After graduation, I went to college, eventually earning a degree in counseling. It is hard, sometimes sad, but helping someone is extremely rewarding.

"No. I'm off today. Just heading to see dad before I leave. Mama is baking pies for this Friday's picnic, and I told her I'd help."

"Yum." She licks her red-covered lips in appreciation. "Is she making her apple pies?"

"Of course," I say with a laugh.

She chuckles and gives me a quick hug, her rose perfume familiar and comforting. "You tell your mama I'll be by tomorrow to help out."

"I will." I turn to continue toward my dad's office. "See you later, Aunt Bev."

The noise from the bar in the motorcycle club my father runs, Dead Man's Curse, slowly fades as I walk down the hallway. This is an old building, built sometime in the early nineteen hundreds. The first bar in this sleepy town. Wood walls. Stiff, dark green carpet. Dim lighting. One of these days, I'll convince my dad to let me remodel the place.

Just the thought makes me chuckle. It's an old argument, one in which he's always victorious. But I am persistent.

Finding his door closed, I knock gently. I hear his anger, deep and gravely, coming from inside the room, his Southern accent growing thicker with each word. I can only make out bits and pieces of the conversation, but it sounds like someone is reneging on a deal.

Never one to get involved with club business, I turn, deciding I'll just give him a call later, when the door opens.

My dad's an imposing man. He isn't overly tall, but he makes up for it in confidence and strength. His biceps bulge as he grips the phone, his other hand clenching and relaxing. His brown eyes are almost black in his anger, only lightening slightly when he sees me.

"I told you I won't pay a cent more then what we've already agreed on," he snarls, waving me toward one of the chairs by his desk. "Absolutely not. If you can't stick with the original terms, I'll just find someone else... What did I just say?! I'm not going to fucking repeat myself. We either still have a deal and my guys will head out to meet yours in a few hours or we don't. The choice is yours."

I sit back in the chair, watching him pace around the room like a caged animal. Whoever is on the other end of the phone isn't saying anything to calm the situation. In fact, it looks like he's deliberately provoking it. My father's breathing quickens, face getting redder by the second.

When there's a quick knock on the door, we both turn to see, my older brother, Brian, known as Mustang in the club, walking in with a frown.

While I take after our mama, with my long, brown hair and willowy figure, my brother definitely looks like our dad. Average height, muscular, self-assured.

My brother eyes Dad for a moment before closing the door and leaning against it. *Fat Mike?* he mouths. Dad nods.

This Fat Mike...what a name...sounds like someone they've had trouble with. At least that's the impression I get from the look of disgust on their faces.

I should get going, I mouth and stand.

Dad holds up a finger. "Fine," he growls into the phone. "We'll meet today, then talk about these *changes* you want to make."

Dad hangs up, aggressively slamming down the receiver. "Bastard."

Taking a deep breath to calm himself, he walks over and pulls me into a hug. "What are you doing, sweetie?"

"Just heading home to help Mama with her baking," I respond, returning the tight embrace. "I wanted to let you know I was leaving."

Squeezing my arms one last time, Dad places a kiss on my forehead before stepping away. "Drive safe. I shouldn't be too long before I head home myself. Tell your mama I'm putting in a request for one of those pies to be just mine."

Laughing, I give my brother a quick hug

just as he seconds the request. "You both know Mama always sets two pies aside just for you."

"Yeah? Then why do I only ever get a slice or two?" my dad asks, shooting a glare at my brother.

Hearing him splutter something about not knowing what he's talking about, I laugh and step out of the office. As I close the door, I hear my brother's voice.

"Fat Mike trying to fuck with our deal?"

"We've never had a problem dealing with the Wicked Rogues, but maybe it's time to cut ties. I don't usually put a lot of stock in rumors, but the shit I hear coming out of that club lately... It's not good."

"I've heard the same."

I worry my bottom lip. I know I shouldn't be listening, but I can't help it.

"We'll continue with our plans, then take our concerns to the club. Put it to a vote." I hear the aggravation, the exhaustion in my dad's voice. "Watch your back tonight. I know Maverick and his guys are cool, but I wouldn't put it past Fat Mike to try some shit."

I step away from the door and make my way through the bar, walking out the front door. My thoughts run over what little I know about the Wicked Rogues, which isn't much.

My dad has always made sure to separate club business and family business. While I know the names of some of the other clubs, I don't know much else.

But the Wicked Rogues... That name has floated around the clubhouse more and more lately, always with sounds of disgust.

My chest tightens as I reach my car. Many times over the years, there have been instances when I felt concern for my family. It feels different this time, though. Even the air around the building feels thicker, the shadows more ominous.

With a last look at the clubhouse, I suppress the shiver running down my spine and climb into the car, hoping my intuition is wrong.

Chapter 3
Maverick

Checking my saddlebag one last time, I nod, confident I have everything I need. This run isn't far, maybe fifteen minutes, but I've learned a lot can happen within a short amount of time.

After securing the latch on the bag, I check my gun harness, pulling out the Glock resting in it. I know this is just a nervous habit, yet can't stop myself from making sure it is loaded and ready to go.

Unfortunately, with the way things have been going lately, the odds of needing my gun are greater than usual.

I place my gun back into my leather strap, then check my phone. It's getting close to the time we need to leave, so I know Smoke and Dodger will be pulling up any moment.

"Hey, Maverick."

Turning, I spot Smoke's younger

brothers, identical triplets Talon, Viper, and Switchblade, heading my way. They've been prospecting for the club for the better part of the last two years, proving themselves time and time again. The club officers will soon discuss patching the three in. But with Fat Mike turning against anyone who doesn't completely agree with him, I'm slightly surprised he hasn't tried to kick out the triplets...or worse.

"Boys," I respond, nodding as they stop in front of me.

"You getting ready to head out?" Talon asks.

Most people aren't able to tell the boys apart, but there are a few slight differences between them.

Talon has a single piercing through the eyebrow above his right eye. It's a small, gold hoop that seems to always catch the light. Switchblade, or Switch, has several piercings: one through his right eyebrow, one through the right nostril, and four in each ear. When the sun hits his face just right, it's almost blinding. Then there is Viper. He has no visible piercings. Just a wicked snake tattoo that comes up from his chest and wraps around the left side of his neck. The head of the snake stares down anyone behind him, the eyes seeming to have a life of their own.

The brothers make quite the impact when they're together, especially since they all have the same mischievous look in their eyes.

Which is vastly different to the hard, cold look in Smoke's.

"Yeah. Smoke and Dodger are riding with me, Stress driving the van with the cases. What are you boys up to?"

"Not sure yet," Switch answers, his smirk promising it'll probably involve getting into trouble. "You ready to see your future brother-in-law?"

I suck in a breath. Hell, I hardly let myself think about her, keeping my mind occupied with other things, but with Switch's question, my brain is immediately filled with gorgeous, brown eyes and silky, auburn hair.

Jenny...

I remember the first time I saw her. I'd just left the grocery store when I heard the most beautiful laugh. Pausing next to my bike,

I looked over and just about dropped my bags.

The woman a few cars down from me was breathtaking. The sparkle in her eyes as she laughed. Her brown hair shining in the sunlight. Smooth, lean legs that disappeared into a pair of shorts that should be illegal. I was so captivated, it took me several minutes to drag my gaze from her and look at the men standing next to her.

The president and VP of the Dead Man's Curse motorcycle club, Brick, and his son, Mustang. As I watched, I quickly saw the resemblance. It was then I remembered hearing Brick had a son *and* a daughter.

Of course, I hightailed it out of the parking lot, not looking back.

Even knowing how dangerous my interest in Brick's daughter is, I can't get her out of my head. I know the man would have my ass if I even breathe in her direction, but I have a feeling it would be worth it.

Jenny...

It's been a few years since that first time I laid eyes on her, but my breath still hitches with even the smallest glimpse.

Of course, over the years, the guys have noticed my interest. So while I've never talked to any of them about her, the nosy bastards seemed to figure everything out.

"Whatever."

At their laughter, I give Talon a good shove.

"*Anyway*... Whatever you guys get into tonight, don't do anything too crazy." I shake my head at their matching grins. "Think about your poor mama. With your brother out with me, you know she's going to worry. Don't give her more to fret over."

"Sure thing, boss man," Talon quips, giving me a mock salute.

Just as I'm about to give him another shove, I pause at the growl Viper releases beside me. He rarely talks. I think I've only heard him speak a handful of times, and that was just a few words. So for him to make any kind of sound means there is something he wants us to notice.

"Well, would ya look at that," Switch

says softly, slightly nodding to the left.

Glancing over, I notice Fat Mike talking with Freddie, our VP. Their expressions are hard, cruel.

"Wonder what that's about?" Talon pulls a notebook from his back pocket, eyes darting around. To the casual observer, it looks like he's lost interest, but I knew better.

"Plotting their next fuckup, I'm sure," Switch grumbles, still watching them out of the corner of his eye.

"Which would be amusing, except their fuckups hurt the rest of us."

We all nod at Talon's assessment. Over the past few years, nothing that had gone wrong seemed to touch Fat Mike or his inner circle, but the rest of us... You'd think we all walked around with big targets on our backs.

Hearing the rumble of bikes, I look over and grin as Smoke and Dodger drive toward the clubhouse. The setting sun twinkles off the chrome of their bikes. They pull up to us and stop, both glancing toward Fat Mike and Freddie, who turn and head back inside without a backward glance.

"I guess we don't get a 'good luck on the meeting'," I mumble. Not that I really expected one. When I joined the club, things were different. Good.

God, I miss that club.

"You can't be shocked the fucks don't care," Dodger snarls.

"No," I sigh as I look at the door to the club, then shake my head before turning back to the guys.

"You two ready?" Both give me a nod, Dodger lighting a cigarette, Smoke walking to his brothers.

I watch the brothers all bump fists before Smoke pulls Viper into a hug. "You guys want to meet up later?" he inquires.

"Sure. We can meet at that bar downtown. What's it called?" Talon asks.

"Brimmers." Switch nods. "That sounds good. I like the beer they have on tap. Plus, we can play a game or two of pool."

"Not to mention the female bartender,"

Smoke throws out.

Switch smirks, waggling his brows.

Viper clears his throat. Turning, I see him looking at me, a question in his gray, piercing eyes.

I nod. "Smoke and I already talked about calling our own meeting. We agree things need to change. But we need to be careful how we go about this, and everyone must agree on what needs done before we move forward."

I pin each of them with a stare, making sure everyone understands. Last thing I need is for anyone to go off half-cocked.

"Where's Stress?" Dodger asks, glancing around the parking lot.

"Last I knew, he was filling up the van, then him and some of the guys were gonna load it up. He should be about ready."

As if conjured up by the conversation, I spot Stress driving the black van around the side of the clubhouse. We make eye contact and exchange nods as he pulls to a stop to wait for us.

"Maybe we should take Fix with us," Smoke suggests.

"You thinking there's going to be trouble?" Dodger growls, taking another long drag from his cigarette.

"What?" Switch looks between them. "With the guys from the DMC?"

"Naw." Smoke shakes his head. "Dead Man's Curse has always been a solid club to do business with. If there's trouble tonight, it won't come from them." Giving me a meaningful look, he continues. "I do feel like something isn't right, though. I just think we should have Fix with us."

I see where he is coming from. If there is anyone I would want at my back, besides the men standing around me now, it would be Fix. He wasn't given that road name for no reason. He sees a problem and fixes it.

If shit hits the fan tonight, we'll need not only another set of eyes, but someone who will do what needs to be done.

Dodge shrugs, glancing my way. "It wouldn't hurt."

I look at Smoke. "Make the call. Tell him we're heading out and to meet us on the road."

As he makes his way into the garage to call Fix, I hold up a finger, letting Stress know it'll be just another minute. When I glance at Dodger and the triplets, I see the concern in their eyes.

"Who are we meeting up with?" Dodger asks, dropping his cigarette, crushing it under the toe of his boot.

"Well, the club's VP is usually there, along with three or four guys. So... Mustang and probably Chopper, Linch, and English. At least that's who showed for the last few meetings." Sighing, I lean back against my bike. "They're all good guys. We've never had trouble with them before. I can't see why today would be any different."

"Unless Fat Mike did something to set them off," Talon suggests.

His comment earns a lot of agreement from the rest of them and a quick nod from Viper, who flicks out one of his knives and begins to spin it in his hand.

I glance toward the garage, seeing Smoke walking our way. "And?" I ask.

"He's on his way. Once I told him what was going on, he immediately headed out the front door."

"Okay." I straighten and swing my leg over my bike. "Let's get this over with." Raising a hand, I make a circular motion and hear Stress rev the van in response. We are as prepared as we are ever going to be.

Smoke and Dodger follow, giving a quick wave to the triplets as we pull out. The boys had made some noise about being left out, but I told them I didn't want to pull up with a huge crew and give Mustang and the others the wrong idea.

Once on the road, I think about seeing Fat Mike and Freddie in conversation. Between that and the secret meeting they had earlier, I can only come to one conclusion. They are up to something, and it's probably not going to be good for the rest of us.

But as Fix pulls out from one of the side streets and falls in behind the van, I release a small grin, the tightening in my chest loosening just a bit. Not enough for me to feel completely comfortable about tonight, but enough that if shit does hit the fan, I like our odds.

Chapter 4
Maverick

It takes us almost twenty minutes to get to the warehouse. Not bad, but it does put us about three minutes late.

So I'm not surprised to find the Dead Man's Curse boys already waiting for us.

Mustang leans against his bike, arms crossed, head tilted slightly as he listens to something one of his guys, Linch, has to say.

Whatever he hears doesn't make him happy. Even at this distance, I see him frown before giving Linch a quick shake of his head. He then straightens from his bike as we pull to a stop a few feet away.

Dismounting, I motion to the other guys to stay put as I make my way toward Mustang, meeting him halfway between our groups, stopping a few feet from each other.

"Maverick."

I know something is up just by the way he says my name. It isn't as if we're friends, but we have been working with each other long enough that I can pick up on his mood just by his tone of voice.

And he is pissed.

Releasing a hiss of air, I nod. "Mustang."

"You're late," he says, glancing around before looking back at me.

"We hit a bit of traffic."

He glances around again, posture stiff, fingers twitching.

"Everything okay?" I question.

"Not sure," Mustang answers, eyes narrowing. "Is it?"

Confused, I glance behind me. All the guys have the same look on their faces...furrowed brow, downturned mouth. Smoke even shrugs slightly. We have absolutely no idea why he's so on edge.

Turning back to Mustang, I glance at his boys standing behind him, noticing they all seem just as tense.

This meeting could seriously go to hell if someone even blinks wrong. And fuck if I know how to defuse the situation. Deciding the best course of action is to stay as calm as possible, I give him a small smile.

"Everything's cool." I gesture toward the van. "We can start loading your cases whenever you're ready. Sound good?"

He studies me for a beat or two, as if trying to find the deception. A drip of sweat trickles down my back as the seconds tick by.

"Yeah," he finally responds, holding up a hand.

One of his guys walks around the corner. Seconds later, I hear an engine and see a gray van pull up. I look at Dodger and give him a nod.

"Aren't you even going to ask how much we got for you?"

Turning back to Mustang, I frown. "How much cash?"

"Yeah."

"Why would I? It's been the same ever

since we started doing business. As far as I know, nothing has changed." That tightness in my chest returns. "Has it?"

I can tell he isn't sure whether to believe me or not. After several moments, he nods and reaches into his back pocket, pulling out the familiar yellow envelope.

As I reach for it, the sound of approaching motorcycles reaches us.

"Who's that?" Mustang growls.

"No idea," I answer slowly, still looking in the direction of the sound. "We should hurry this up and get out of here."

"I don't think we have time," he says. "Are they with you?"

"No. I figured they were with you."

We glance at each other. Fuck, this is going to get messy. I can feel it. And I might be crazy, but a few of those engines sound familiar. Unfortunately, I am proven right as the bikes pull around the corner.

"Maverick...," Smoke hisses, slamming the van doors.

I don't even need to look at him to know his face is twisted in anger. It probably matches the look I try to suppress when I see who pulls up behind us.

Fat Mike pulls to stop not far from where I stand. With him is Freddie, our VP, and another of his followers, an idiot named Brash. I've never liked the guy. He's a fight first, ask questions later type, and I can't stand people like that.

"Boys." Fat Mike's gruff voice echoes in the stillness that has descended over us.

"Prez," I acknowledge. "We're just finishing up."

"Then I'm just in time," he sneers. "I have a little business with Mustang before we finalize today's transaction."

Listening to him act like a businessman makes me cringe.

"And what business is that?" Mustang asks calmly. The only sign he is uneasy is the slight shift in his stance, almost like preparing himself. Smoke and the boys, along with the DMC guys, stand around the two vans, waiting to see how this plays out.

"I informed Brick the price for doing business was going up. Now, he said he wouldn't agree to any changes in our agreement, even though I *strongly* suggested he reconsider. I hoped he had a change of heart and sent you with *all* the money I requested." Fat Mike glances toward the vans, then back at Mustang, sneering. "If not, we're going to take those guns back with us."

"They're already loaded in our van." Mustang's eyes narrow as he glares at Fat Mike. "Regardless, I have the money we agreed on. The same amount I bring every time. Brick said nothing about any changes. So, until I'm told otherwise..." He holds out the envelope, staring straight into Fat Mike's eyes.

I want to jump in and say something, stop the train wreck that is about to happen, but I know if I do, it'll only make things worse.

"Yes, well..." He forces out a smile, taking the envelope from Mustang's hand. "I'll definitely be talking with Brick to...renegotiate our arrangement."

"I'll be sure to let him know to expect

your call."

We all stand there for another second before Mustang signals to his guys to mount up. The DMC van pulls away from ours, stopping over by their bikes, the driver leaning out to talk to Mustang.

Fat Mike watches them as he slides the envelope into his back pocket, his movements slow and deliberate. "Hey, Mustang?!" he yells.

Mustang turns, a slight frown on his face. "Yeah?"

"Give your dad a message for me."

"What's that?"

Fat Mike smiles, eyes remaining cold. "I always get what I'm owed... One way or another."

Time seems to slow. I see him pull out his gun, an almost maniacal laugh escaping him as he pulls the trigger. Mustang dodges to the right, yelling out and rolling behind their van.

Someone shouts behind me before more gunshots ring out. I dive behind a dumpster, covering my head when a few bullets ping off it.

Everyone starts yelling, their voices barely audible over the sounds of gunfire. I pull out my Glock and peek around the side of the dumpster, seeing Dodger go down.

"Dodger!" I roar.

Hunched over, Fix races forward to grab his arm, pulling Dodger behind our van. After several minutes, Smoke leans around the van, giving me a thumbs up. I blow out the breath I hadn't even known I was holding.

How many others have been injured? Everything had gone to hell so quickly, nobody had been able to duck for cover before the bullets started flying.

I hear shouting coming from where Mustang and his guys are pinned down. Glancing that way, I can tell some had been hit, but none of the injures look fatal. And our guys are all safe in the van.

Thank fuck.

A few pings against the dumpster had me pulling back again. I hear Fat Mike curse as the DMC members all start shooting in his direction. The sound is deafening as I huddle there, my gun clenched in my hand as I wait for a break in the chaos. Not that I want to shoot anyone, but if it comes down to me or them, well... I plan on going home today.

Fuck Fat Mike. Fuck his kiss-ass followers. And fuck the way they think things should be done.

Hearing engines, I peek around the dumpster, smiling slightly. Brilliant. The DMC guys used the barrage of gunfire for cover to get to their bikes and get the hell out of there.

With a few of their members bringing up the rear and shooting wildly over their shoulders, they pull away, their engines screaming as they push them as fast as they can go.

Fat Mike steps out from behind his bike, continuing to shoot at them until his gun is empty.

Slowly stepping out from behind the dumpster, I tuck my gun back into my holster, Smoke doing the same as he moves from behind the van.

"Who's hurt?" I call out.

Smoke blows out a breath. "Dodger was shot in the arm. It was a through and through, but we're pretty sure it caught the bone. Fix put a tourniquet on it until we can get him to Doc. Stress' face and neck got cut up pretty bad when the van's window shattered." Smoke shakes his head, glancing toward Fat Mike, lackeys in tow, who makes his way toward us. "We stopped them from bleeding, but there are still a few big pieces of glass in his cheeks. We'd rather have Doc remove those."

"What the fuck?!" Fat Mike yells.

Some would think he's angry because he's concerned about our injuries. However, we all know that's not the case.

"There were six of us. *Six*. How the fuck did they get away? What were you idiots doing? Cowering like a bunch of babies?"

"It's not like we prepared for a shootout," Smoke argues. "What the fuck was that about anyway?"

"That was me taking care of business. It's not like I can trust you guys to do it." He throws up his hands in frustration. "Fuck. A few bullets go flying and you all run for cover. Disgusting. At least Freddie and Brash shot back. I think we even got one or two of those fuckers. But with all of us here, we should have bodies lying over there." Fat Mike shakes his head, glancing at Freddie and Brash. "Let's get back to the club so we can figure out how to clean up this fucking mess."

"What do you want us to do?" I ask.

"Load up and get back to the fucking clubhouse," he snarls, then turns and heads toward his bike. "You guys had better hope we figure out a way to deal with this," he shoots over his shoulder before the three of them mount up and peel away.

"What. The. Fuck?" Smoke grinds out.

Shrugging, I walk toward Fix, who leans against the side of the van, cigarette in his mouth.

"We need to put a stop to this," he says. "He almost got us fucking killed this time."

Smoke snorts. "Honestly, I think he was actually disappointed we weren't."

Sighing, I shake out my hands as adrenalin begins to leave my body. I've been in similar situations before, but never without being prepared for the possibility. This was too close. Too real.

"We need to get out of here." I glance around. "The gunfire might have been heard by someone. Smoke, go ahead and take off. As soon as you get back, call Doc and tell him what happened." Smoke nods, hurrying toward his bike. Looking at Fix, I nod toward the bikes. "Help me load Dodger's and my bike into the van. I'll drive it back. I'm sure Stress is in no position to do it."

He smirks. "You know he probably would if we asked him."

"Yeah, he would." I exhale. "Let's get back. I have a feeling the night isn't over."

As we load up the bikes and get on the road, all I can think about is that this could have been the end for all of us. I'm sure we'll hear from Brick soon enough. There's no way he'll let this amount of disrespect go. Hell, I wouldn't, either

Something needs to be done about Fat

Mike and his followers. I'm certain there will be more bloodshed before everything is said and done. But we need to protect our club. Even if the risk is coming from within it.

Chapter 5
Jenny

Chaos.

That's what we walk into when we show up at the clubhouse.

I had just started watching a movie, ready to relax after helping my mom get the last pie into the oven, when I heard my dad's phone ring.

His outburst shortly after made me jump off the couch and stride into the kitchen.

"Who was hurt?" he barks into the phone, pulling on his vest and grabbing his keys. "*Fuck*. Is he okay?... What the fuck happened?"

I couldn't hear the other end of the conversation, but it had my dad racing toward the front door, skidding to a stop when my mom stepped in front of him.

"What happened?" she asked, eyes

pleading.

Even before my dad answered, I knew. His clenched fists, pained expression, rapid breathing. Those are his tells. Something happened to Mustang. Seeing the shadow descend over my mom's face, I knew she'd come to the same conclusion, especially when she grabbed her purse and coat before my dad even answered her.

"There was an incident. Everyone's alive, but Brian was hurt."

Hearing my dad use my brother's real name, not his road name, showed just how upset he was.

The next ten minutes were a blur as we made our way to the club. On the way, dad told us that Chopper had already called his friend, David, who's a doctor. Him and dad grew up together and have always been close. David is always willing to swing by when anyone from the club calls.

Trying to stay strong for my mom, I kept my worries to myself as we pulled up to the club. Getting out of the car, everything was quiet. Nobody would know the bedlam going on inside...until you opened the door.

Angry proclamations... Swearing... Confusion...

Dad grabs my mom's hand and places his other hand against my back as we work our way through the throng and toward one of the meeting rooms.

Inside, we find several of the guys...bleeding, angry. And on a table in the center lies Mustang, blood covering the side of his head and dripping onto the table. Mom gasps as we rush over.

"I'm fine," Mustang says, voice hoarse.

"Fine? You have blood all over your head," Mom exclaims, hands shaking slightly as she reaches out and grabs one of his.

"Seriously, Ma. I'm okay."

"He'll be fine," David says, reaching into his bag and pulling out several bandages and gauze pads, followed by hydrogen peroxide. "He's lucky. The bullet just grazed his head. It did take the tip of his ear clean off, but I think that may improve his looks."

"Ha-ha-ha. Very funny," Mustang slurs.

At Mom's questioning look, David smiles. "I gave him some morphine to take the edge off. I need to put in a few stitches and clean him up, then you guys can take him home."

"But...," I start, looking over the table. "But there's so much blood."

"Head wounds, even minor ones, bleed a lot. Also, Mustang hit the ground pretty hard, then scrambled to get away, severely scraping up his neck, shoulder, and upper back. I basically had to scrub those wounds to get the dirt and gravel out, so that could account for some of the blood." He pauses, giving me a gentle smile. "Your brother is going to be just fine, Jenny. Promise."

"Thank you for getting here so quickly," my dad utters. These are the first words out of him since we got here.

Turning toward him, I suck in a breath. I've never seen him look so...murderous. Face red, teeth grinding, veins in his neck bulging. I can tell it's taking all his willpower to keep from storming out of the room and going on the warpath.

"Of course." David smiles, going back to stitching up Mustang's ear. My brother is slightly dozing, feeling no pain, eyes unfocused as he listens to our mom telling him he is going to be okay.

Dad looks around the room, eyes narrowed. Linch sits to our left. He complains to a few other members as his wife, Meg, places a bandage on his arm. Chopper sits on the right. He has a nasty cut on his cheek that looks like it's going to need stitches. He keeps pushing English's hand away, the man trying to put a rag to the cut as he tells him to quit being an ass.

The knowledge that everyone is going to be okay doesn't seem to cool my dad's rising temper, and knowing what is to come, I decide to get mom out of there.

"Come on, Mama," I say softly, giving her arm a gentle tug. "Let's get some food together for everyone."

That's all it takes to get my mom moving. She is a comforter, a provider. Making sure everybody has food is what she would do.

The kitchen's just down the hall from the meeting room. With the paper-thin walls, we can hear when my dad finally loses it.

"What the *fuck* happened?!"

We don't overhear what is said, but we definitely hear my dad's reaction to it.

"Fat Mike shot you?! *Fucking hell!*... He said what?... *Dammit!* Well, he ain't getting shit but a bullet to the head now..."

Glancing at my mom, she purses her lips and shakes her head. We both know we shouldn't be hearing this, club business is private, but it can't be helped. As mom places the last of the sandwiches onto the plater, I grab a few bags of chips from the cupboard.

"Who the fuck was there with him?... That's it?... What did Maverick say?" I've heard the name before but had never met the man. From what I can tell, though, he's someone my dad respects. "And he seemed surprised to see Fat Mike show up?" He sounds a lot calmer. Still angry, but his tempter isn't at atomic levels anymore. "Fine. If you think we can trust him, I'll page Maverick and see if he calls. If he does, I'll set something up for tomorrow."

Both of us grabbing a platter and a bag of chips, I follow my mom out of the kitchen and into the meeting room. I take in the grim looks on the faces. This isn't over. Whoever Maverick is, I hope he can help settle this without anybody else getting hurt.

Chapter 6
Maverick

Taking a drink from my beer, I watch Doc bounce between Dodger and Stress. The boys sit at one of the tables in the bar, nursing a drink, still covered in blood and dirt. Their appearance is a reminder of how close the club had come to losing more brothers.

Doc places the last stitch in Dodger's arm, then bandages the wound, making sure it is completely covered. He places a sling around Dodger's neck, situating his arm in it. He takes a step back, nods in satisfaction, then turns to Stress and grabs a large pair of tweezers from his bag in order to take the glass out of his face.

Everyone is, angry, confused. Their voices are a combination of hushed whispers and aggressive questions, all blending together and adding to the already tense mood.

It isn't the first time one of us had been shot, and I doubt it'll be the last. But each time is like we all share in that person's pain. Well, *almost* all of us.

Turning my head when the front door opens, I watch Fat Mike, Freddie, and a few of their lackies make their way into the clubhouse. Everyone stops talking and turns their way.

"What the hell you doing here, Doc?" Fat Mike growls, making his way to the bar and grabbing a bottle of beer.

Never taking his eyes off Stress as he pulls another piece of glass from his cheek, Doc clicks his tongue. "I'm fixing up your club members. Making sure they're okay."

"Why?" He glances at Dodger and Stress with a look of contempt. "They're the ones who didn't do their job. Let them bleed. Maybe they'll learn to shoot first next time. Instead of standing there like the worthless bastards they are."

Doc slams his tweezers onto the table and glares at Fat Mike as he grabs bandages. "My job is to take care of these men, regardless of how or why they get injured."

He turns back to Stress, voice softening. "I got all the glass out. Make sure you keep the cuts clean and let me know if they get infected." At Stress' nod and whispered thanks, Doc reaches for his bag.

"You'll treat, or not treat, whoever I fucking tell you to. This is my club. If I want one of the members to learn a lesson, that's what's going to happen. You got it?"

"As long as I work for this club, I will take care of these guys. That is what I was brought in for. I'm not about to change now." Doc stuffs the last of his supplies into his bag, his anger and frustration evident. "If you won't allow me to do my job, I'm not going to be here."

"If that's how you feel, Doc," Fat Mike sneers, "don't let the door hit you on the way out."

Stunned silence descends over the room, everyone shocked. Doc has been helping us for years, no questions asked. What are we going to do now? How will we find another doctor like him?

Doc's eyes narrow, jaw clenching as he stares at Fat Mike, who takes a swig of his beer, acting unconcerned.

After a few more minutes of glaring at each other, Fat Mike takes one last drink and slams his bottle onto the bar, looking at his men. "Let's get out of here. I can't stand to be in this room right now."

His followers laugh as they trail after him like the good little lambs they are.

Doc stands there for a moment, staring at the door they'd just walked through. Then he sighs and turns back to us. "Sorry, guys. You all know I'd do anything for you. I just... I can't do this anymore. Not with him in charge." Grabbing his bag, Doc looks around once more before making his way toward the door. "I'm sorry," he mumbles, then slips outside.

I meet Storm's eyes. "Talk to him, Maverick. Tell him to give us a little time."

Nodding, I stride to the door and swing it open, stepping out into the chilly night. I look around, seeing Doc placing his bag into the trunk of his car and slamming it shut.

I pick up my pace. "Wait, Doc."

He turns, a resigned look on his face. "Maverick, I know what you're going to say, but–"

I hold up my hand. "Just let me get this out." At his nod, I sigh. "Look, I know things have been shit lately. And we both know who is the cause of most of the problems. We just need you to give us a little time."

"Time?"

"Yeah. We have some things in the works. Don't give up on us just yet." I run a hand through my hair, feeling every one of my forty years. "I don't know how much time, but it won't be long. I promise you. The club will be different soon. Better."

His eyes search mine, as if looking for some answers. He finally gives me a nod and squeezes my arm before getting into his car and pulling out of the parking lot.

Sighing, I tilt my head back and close my eyes. Could this day get any more stressful?

The thought had just left my mind when my pager vibrates in my pocket. "Dammit," I hiss. *What now?*

I pull it out, pausing as an unknown number flashes across the screen. I normally don't call numbers I don't know, but something urges me to call this one.

I walk into the garage and close the door, then make my way to the back and grab the phone. Punching in the number, I wait, listening to the ringing, as I try to figure out who it could be.

"Hello," I respond when the call connects. "I got a page from this number."

"Maverick?" the deep voice growls. It's familiar, but I can't place it. "It's Brick. We need to talk."

Shit!

I lean back against the workbench. "Yes, we do," I answer simply. I have no idea why he's calling me.

"Can I trust you not to pull any of the bullshit that happened today?"

"Yes. What happened today was—"

Brick grunts, interrupting me. "Five o'clock tomorrow at The Empty Shot in Livermore. Come alone."

"Yes, sir."

He disconnects the call before I can say anything else. I blow out a breath and hang up. Brick sounded pissed, and for good reason. He's probably going to expect some answers from me. Guess I need to get the guys together before I head out so I know what to tell him.

Hanging my head, I feel my body sag with tiredness.

There is no question. Fat Mike and his lackies need to be dealt with, and I am certain there will be more blood spilled before this is over.

Chapter 7
Maverick

The next day, the brothers and I meet at a place Fat Mike and the rest don't frequent because it is owned by three brothers, one of whom is out and proud of it. Something Fat Mike refuses to be around, which works for us. We had helped them out a time or two, which means we can use their back room whenever needed.

I had hoped we could come up with something simple and straight to the point. However, the guys spend the first hour and a half bitching about anything and everything Fat Mike has pulled. By the time we finally get down to talking about the main problem and throwing out ideas about how to deal with it, I just want it to be done.

We have reached a decision, though. Fat Mike and his followers, some I have known for more years than I care to think about, have to be eliminated, and it needs to happen in one swoop; otherwise we leave ourselves open to retaliation.

It's kill or be killed.

At the end of the almost three-hour long meeting, we all leave with a heaviness in our chests that hadn't been there before. It's nice to finally have a direction, a promise of an end to the shitty situation our club has found itself in, but what we need to do is going to come with a heavy price.

I just hope everyone is prepared for that. Truthfully, I'm not sure I am. But this needs to be done if we are to survive.

Not wanting to be late for my meeting with Brick, I rush out. Fix and Smoke argued that they were coming with me. That I needed somebody to watch my back.

I made my case, telling them I thought it would be best if I went alone. Show Brick I wasn't worried about meeting with him.

Even though I am.

It took some doing, but they finally relented. Although, with the looks they gave each other right before I left, I wouldn't be surprised if they left five minutes after I did, following at a distance.

Glancing in my side mirror as I curve through Altamont Pass, I snort. Sure enough, a few miles back, two bikes come around the curve. I'm annoyed, but also happy to know I have support on this.

Settling in to the ride, my mind turns over what could happen today. After several minutes of going over the *what ifs*, most of which are not pleasant to think about, I decide to switch gears to something a lot more...enjoyable.

Jenny...

The likelihood of seeing her today is nonexistent, yet I can't help but imagine how fantastic it would be. Maybe I'll get up the nerve to talk to her this time. Smirking at the fact I still need to build up the courage to talk to a pretty girl, I pull off the freeway and make my way toward the bar.

I know I'm early. Maybe I'll be able to get my thoughts in order before Brick gets here.

But as I park, I notice two bikes by the front entrance and sigh. Time's up.

A sudden feeling of unease washes

through me. I begin to wonder if it was a good idea to come alone. I should probably wait for Smoke and Fix to pull in, tell them I changed my mind about them joining me, but I just can't shake the feeling showing up by myself is better. Show Brick I'm a man of my word.

Sucking in a breath, I dismount and make my way to the door, running a hand through my hair. With each step, I remind myself how I've always had a good relationship with Dead Man's Curse, hoping Brick takes that into consideration.

I reach for the door handle, then pause. "I hope I'm not wrong about them," I whisper before pulling open the door.

It isn't hard to spot Brick, even in the dim lighting. Besides being built, the man just has an aura around him that demands respect. My eyes stray to Mustang sitting next to him, not surprised to see him here. What does make me pause is the large bandage covering his right ear. I knew Fat Mike had taken some shots at him. I just hadn't realized he'd been hit. Both men lean toward each other, talking in low voices. As I walk up, they straighten, their hard gazes taking me in as I grab a chair across from them and sit down.

I nod. "Brick. Mustang."

"Maverick," Brick responds, while Mustang just returns my nod. There is a tense moment as we sit there, Brick flagging down a server to bring us some beers and chips with salsa.

It isn't until after we each have a cold beer in front of us and take a swig that Brick breaks the silence.

"The fuck happened?"

I take another drink to give myself time to formulate a response. "You know what happened. It wasn't planned. Hell, I didn't even know Fat Mike tried to change our agreement. It's not like he tells me shit."

Brick is quiet, his gaze drilling into me as I talk. It makes me want to fidget with the label of the bottle in my hands. I'm not exactly sure what kind of answer he's looking for, but I am not about to go into detail about what the club is going through at the moment. The only reason I had agreed to meet with him was because our problems have spilled over into his club.

"Listen, I'm not sure what you want me to say. The situation quickly went to shit and there was no way to fucking stop it."

"I had a meeting with my men this afternoon," Brick starts. "A lot of the guys want to be done with it and fucking end Fat Mike. After the recent bullshit, I'm not entirely opposed to the idea."

I open my mouth, not entirely sure how to respond to that. All I know is we can't afford a war with the DMC on top of everything else. Cursing Fat Mike once more, I try to think of something to say to get Brick to hold off on that right now.

He holds up his hand. "I'm not saying that's what we're going to do, but your club has a serious fucking problem, Maverick. Now, I don't know what is going on and I don't care. But I've heard rumors that don't sit well with me, especially ones concerning a club I have dealings with."

I watch him take a drink of his beer. He isn't saying anything that surprises me. Truthfully, considering everything, I feel like

Brick is being pretty calm. The only clue he isn't is the anger in his eyes. The need to choose my next words carefully is extremely important.

"I hear you, Brick, and I completely understand. The Rogues are going through some shit right now. But everything should be worked out soon." I down the last of my beer. "We just need a little time to figure things out."

He studies me for a moment, then nods and glances at Mustang, some of his anger fading. "Good. I've always considered you a trustworthy man, Maverick. That's the only reason we're sitting here. However, if your house doesn't get in order soon, we'll be forced to step in and take care of it for you. Understand?"

I nod. "Yeah."

"Good. I truly hope it doesn't come to that. I don't think it would be good for either club."

"I agree."

He leans back in his chair and taps the table with his fingers. "Let me know once it's done, then I'll decide if we're able to continue to do business."

Knowing a dismissal when I hear one, I stand, pull some cash out of my pocket and place it onto the table, then walk out of the bar. My mind goes over everything that needs to be done, as well as all the possible outcomes, both good and bad. Just the thought of going to war with the DMC is unimaginable, although I have a funny feeling Fat Mike wouldn't be upset about it in the least. He'd probably see it as a way of getting rid of some of his club's "dead weight".

Shaking my head in disgust, I make my way through the parking lot, stopping short when I see a familiar, black Camaro pull in. A small smile pulls on my lips.

Jenny...

Chapter 8
Jenny

It took everything I had this morning to convince my dad to let me tag along today. I knew I couldn't be there while they had their meeting, but I told them I'd hit the mall while they were busy, then show up a half-hour later.

Wanting to go with them isn't something I'd normally do, but finding out they were going to The Empty Shot, where they served the best pulled pork sliders and chili cheese fries, had my mouth watering.

Of course, the fact they were meeting with Maverick may have had a bit to do with it. Even though I've never met or even seen the man, what I'd heard about him added to my desire to be there.

So here I am, pulling into The Empty Shot's parking lot. I know Dad told me to wait until he paged me before showing up, but I just couldn't wait anymore, the excitement too great.

Glancing around the parking lot, I see my dad's and brother's bikes sitting in front. As much as the sight of the bikes sitting next to each other, gleaming in the bright sunlight, is calming, images of my brother covered in blood still overwhelm me. The thought of how close we'd come to losing him makes my stomach ache.

Giving myself a little shake, I attempt to push the thoughts out of my mind. "Mama and Dad raised me to be stronger than that," I whisper, searching for a place to park. It was then I notice the most gorgeous man I've ever seen.

I suck in a breath as he stops walking and looks my way. I can't see his eyes because of the black sunglasses he has on, but the rest of him is tall, built, and droolworthy. The well-worn jeans hug his legs. His black shirt stretches tightly across his chest and abs, his black leather vest completing the look. Tattoos peek out from the t-shirt sleeves, and the confident way he holds himself just makes me want to introduce myself.

When my gaze travels back to his face, I notice the smile tugging at the corner of his mouth. Fuck. He totally caught me staring at him.

Biting my lip, I pull into a parking spot and turn off the engine. I take a deep breath and grab my purse, opening the door and stepping into the crisp air.

"Nice car."

I spin around, a shiver rolling down my spine when I see him standing there, my cheeks heating.

The first thing I notice is his roguish smile. Then the steel-blue eyes I could stare into for hours. I send up a silent thank you that he'd taken off his sunglasses. He doesn't hold himself in a cocky way. Doesn't act like he knows how hot he is. I'd met enough guys like that in the past. This guy, though, exuded confidence. It was sexy as hell.

Hearing him let out a soft chuckle, I blink, looking back at his face. "W-What?" I ask.

"I said you have a real nice car."

"Oh..." I glance over my shoulder at it, then back at him. "Thanks. It was my first big purchase. I mean, I've bought stuff before. This was the first car I've ever bought, though. It was all banged up, so I got it for a steal, then my dad and I spent the last several years rebuilding it. It's almost done. There are a few minor things that need to be replaced. Shouldn't take too much longer to get the last few parts we need."

Stopping, I take a deep breath and shake my head. "And I don't know why I told you all that. I'm sure you aren't really interested. So... Yeah... Um, thank you for the compliment."

If I could smack my face and force myself to shut up, I would. Nothing like a little word vomit in front of the hottest guy I've ever seen.

"I don't mind. You've done a really good job. You don't meet many women who know their way around a car. It's hot."

"Yeah?"

"Yeah."

We both stand there, smiling at each other. The need to be closer to him has me taking a small step forward, breathing in the intoxicating smell of leather, oil, and...him.

"Jenny!"

I jerk back and look at the door of the bar, seeing Mustang standing there, frown on his face, narrowed eyes bouncing back and forth between me and the man in front of me.

"Um, I gotta..." I slightly nod at my brother.

"Yeah. I'm sure your dad is waiting."

My brow furrows. "How did you know I'm here to see my dad?"

He grins. "The family resemblance is uncanny. Plus, I've seen you with your dad and brother before." He quickly holds a hand up. "In passing. Nothing stalkerish."

I laugh. "Well, that's good. I've never had a stalker before, but I don't imagine it would go over well with my dad and brother."

"I would think not."

"*Jenny!*"

Looking toward my brother again, I see him wave a hand at me to hurry up. "Just a second, *Brian*!" I yell with a grin, the use of his real name causing his frown to deepen into a truly impressive scowl. Knowing I don't have long before he storms across the lot, I look back at the man in front of me. "You know my name. I think it's only polite I get yours."

"Well, I'm nothing if not polite," he jokes. "I'm Maverick. Well, my given name is Chris. But everyone calls me Maverick."

I can't stop the large smile from spreading across my face. I can finally put a face to the name I had heard so often.

"Well, Maverick..." I love how his name rolls off my tongue. "It's nice to meet you."

"It's nice to meet you, too, Jenny," he utters in a low voice, causing my pulse to quicken.

Stealing a glance toward my brother, I see him take a step toward us. My time is almost up.

"Let me see your hand," I say quickly, reaching into my purse and pulling out a pen.

His eyebrow quirks as he slowly holds out his hand. I flip it over, palm up, and write my number on it.

Releasing his hand, I smile. "Just in case you want to call. Talk about cars or something."

Grinning, he reaches for the pen and my hand. I suck in a quick breath as he writes his number on my palm, his thumb rubbing my skin lightly, tingles shooting up my arm.

He gives my hand a gentle squeeze before releasing it and handing back my pen. "Just in case." He smiles, nodding toward the bar. "You best get in there. I think your brother's not happy with us talking."

I snort. "We're just talking. There's nothing for him to get upset about."

He doesn't respond, just gives me another breathtaking smile. Glancing at his hand, he starts to take a step toward me, then thinks better of it as my brother stops feet from us, arms crossed, nostrils flared.

"Maverick," Mustang practically growls.

"Mustang," he responds, nodding at him before shooting me a quick wink. "Have a good evening, Jenny."

E.F. Rose

"You, too, Maverick."

Watching him turn and walk away, I can't help but let my gaze slide down to his ass. And what a fine ass, too.

"Really, Jenny?" Mustang moans. "Of all the guys in the world... Dad is going to lose his shit, probably lock you in your room with a guard twenty-four/seven."

"We were just talking." I insist, even though I know that won't matter to Dad. Looking down at the number on my hand, I lightly rub my thumb across it, then look back at my brother as we start walking toward the door. "I'm allowed to talk to whomever I want. Plus, I've heard you guys talk about Maverick. It's always seemed like you all thought highly of him."

"Yes, you can talk to who you want, but this couldn't be worse timing." Mustang touches my arm before we get to the door, stopping me. "Listen, I'm not going to tell you who to talk to. Hell, I like Maverick. But his club is going through some shit right now, and I just don't want to see you get wrapped up in it."

Seeing the worry in my brother's eyes, I smile and touch his cheek. "I admit I want to spend time with him. We're just going to talk. Get to know each other. I'll be careful. Promise."

"Okay. But you know you're going to have to do more than promise to be careful with dad. It's going to take some doing to get him to agree to this."

"Well, if you tell him *you're* okay with it—"

He holds up both hands, stepping back, shaking his head. "Oh, no. I'm not getting involved in this. I'm going to order another beer, sit down, and watch the fireworks."

"Thanks a lot." I shove him, making him laugh.

"Seriously, though, Jenny. Make sure he knows if he does you wrong, there will be a whole line of us waiting to deal with him." He holds the door open for me.

Rolling my eyes, I walk into the bar. I know they will be protective, but nothing is going to stop me from talking to Maverick.

I can't wait to learn all I can about him.

Chapter 9
Maverick

It's been five days since I'd met with Brick and Mustang.

Five days since I'd finally met Jenny, exchanging numbers. We've talked every night since. With each conversation, I fall for her more and more. I already thought she was the most beautiful woman I'd ever seen, but I quickly realized her beauty shown just as brightly on the inside. She is amazing.

It's also been five days since my brothers and I decided it was time to deal with Fat Mike and his followers.

So it's been equal parts wonderful and ulcer-inducing. I want to get to know Jenny, but with what is going on in the club, I hesitate to make any plans. The last thing I want is for her to get caught in the middle.

There's a barbeque scheduled at the clubhouse tomorrow. After a lot of back and forth, we've decided to confront Fat Mike then.

Making my way up to my room, I run over our plans. Truthfully, all we had worked out was we'd tell Fat Mike why we can't allow the club to keep going the way it's been going. After that, well... We'll see what happens.

I pull my pager from my pocket as I walk into my room, smiling at the page from Jenny. Sitting on the bed, I grab the phone from its cradle on my nightstand and dial her number, leaning back against the headboard.

"Hello," she says, her soft voice relaxing me.

"Hi. How was your day?"

"Good. I spent it helping Mama around the house. How was your day?"

"It was good. Busy." I rest my head against the headboard. "We have some things coming up. Hopefully everything will calm down soon."

She hasn't asked me what's going on, but I know Jenny's aware something is happening. I've tried to steer our conversations away from the club, but since she's been in this life since birth, she can probably pick up on what I'm *not* saying. Sometimes her tone of voice when we talk conveys worry.

As much as I don't want her concerned, it's kind of nice to know someone cares. I've never experienced that from a woman before.

We only talk for about twenty minutes. She makes me promise to call her after the barbeque. I want to tell her everything will be okay, but I can't bring myself to lie. So I just promise I'll call.

As I hang up, I release a harsh sigh.

This whole situation sucks. I want nothing more than to just skip tomorrow. Unfortunately, that's not an option. Things have gone too far, and I know something must change.

And it suddenly seems more important than it was before. Cleaning up the club isn't just for us anymore. It is for the relationship I want with Jenny. I need to make this a safe place for her.

I just hope when the dust settles, I haven't lost her in the process.

It's almost eight in the evening when the barbeque starts winding down. The day has flown by, but that could just be my nerves. I feel like I am doing pretty good at keeping it together, although I can't say the same for all the guys.

Stress lived up to his road name. I'm thankful the night is almost over because if I have to watch him pace around another minute, I am going to shoot him.

Smoke, on the other hand, acted like it was any other day. He's spent most of the day over by the bar, flirting with several women, laughing with everyone, as if he doesn't have a care in the world. I know differently, though. The tightening around his eyes and the occasional tick in his jaw are tells. All signs he's not as calm as he seems.

I watch Dodger walk his wife and son out. They are the last family to head home, leaving only club members.

Seemingly unconsciously, we've split up

into two groups—Fat Mike and his followers chilling out back; me and the rest of the Rogues in the bar.

Even though the back door leading to the yard is down the hall, I can still hear the obnoxious yelling coming from outside. They've been hitting the bottle hard, but I don't let that fool me. This isn't going to be an easy fight. Most of those guys have been in fights all their lives. Being drunk won't stop them. The most we can hope for is that the alcohol will make them a bad shot.

I glance around the room. Most of the guys watch me, the weight of their gazes weighing me down.

Squaring my shoulders, I finish my beer and stand just as Dodger walks back into the room, closing the door behind him.

"We good?" I ask.

"All clear, boss."

Everyone stands. I hear the sound of metal on metal as guns are checked. There is no talking, no joking around.

"Is Fat Mike still in the back?" I ask

Smoke as he leans against the bar.

"Yeah."

Nodding, I look around the room. "Okay." I make eye contact with each of the men. "Fat Mike and his followers have been breaking our club apart. We've lost members, business, respect. We're all sick of it. It's time to clean house."

At the grunts of agreement, we all head down the hall toward the back entrance. I feel my skin tingle with nerves. We know this needs to happen, but I don't think any of us are truly prepared for it.

But as my hand lands on the doorknob, I feel a calm rush through me. Whatever happens has been a long time coming. I have to believe we will come out on top.

I'm not surprised to see Fat Mike and his men gathered in the back of the yard, the men laughing at his bad jokes, agreeing with his shit ideas.

Freddie, Skeeter, and Brash were some of the first to turn against the rest of the club in the name of "making things better". At least that was the original excuse Fat Mike gave for the changes he started making. The rest of them fell into line over time.

Then there is Poot, who leans against a tree, listening. I'm not entirely sure whose side he's on. Guess we'll find out soon enough.

"Maverick, did everyone clear out?" Fat Mike questions.

Stopping behind one of the picnic benches, I nod. "Yeah."

"Good. I'm glad you're all here because I have an announcement to make." He grins smugly, looking around like he is just about to give us the answer to all our problems.

Glancing to my side, I notice Smoke glaring at Fat Mike, almost daring him to make a move.

"Tick called me—"

"The president of the Jackals?" Dodger interrupts.

"Yes," he grinds out, obviously annoyed. "After talking for a while, I've decided it's going to be in our best interest to merge the two clubs."

"What the fuck?!"

"Absolutely not!"

"How is that a good idea?!"

Voices shoot out like bullets around me, everyone getting more pissed by the minute. Tick is known for his violent and deadly nature. Joining them wouldn't just be a bad idea. It would mean death to the Wicked Rogues.

Holding up a hand, I wait until everyone quiets before focusing on Fat Mike. "And why would you think that would be in the club's best interest?"

"Well..." He drags the word out, like I'm an idiot. "They're a bigger club. They have more money and deal with more lucrative businesses. Why *wouldn't* it be a good idea to join them?"

"Maybe because they're a group of psychopaths," Smoke spits out. "Maybe because some of those *lucrative businesses* you mentioned are rumored to be human trafficking, black market shit. I'm sure there are more reasons, but I think those are enough."

Fat Mike sneers at him. "Worried about a little illegal business, Smoke? How the fuck do you think *we've* been making our money? Selling candy?"

"There's a *huge* difference between selling guns and selling people! I refuse to be aligned with anyone who thinks they're the same."

"And *that*..." Fat Mike jabs a finger at Smoke, "shows how weak you are. This whole club is infested with pansies. Well, not as many as there used to be." He and his followers laugh, then he turns to Freddie. "We took care of that, didn't we?"

"We sure did."

"The fuck you guys say?" I ask. Subconsciously, I knew they had been getting rid of members. A part of me hoped there was another explanation. That he hadn't gone to that extreme. Guess I now know the truth.

"I've been meaning to get rid of the dead weight around here for a while now. Even if Tick hadn't told me I had to get rid of some 'problem areas' in order to merge, I would have done it anyway."

"So... What? You chased them off, got some put in jail, what?" Dodger growls.

Out of the corner of my eye, I notice Fix edge around our group, eyes fixed on the men in front of us. He holds his gun in his right hand, grip relaxed, but I know how fast he can aim and shoot.

"It definitely started like that." Fat Mike's rough voice drew my attention back to him. "But there were a few who just didn't want to fucking leave. So..." He shrugs. "I took care of them."

"Meaning?" I ask.

"I promised Tick I'd get rid of the trash. So whoever I couldn't frame or convince to leave, I put two rounds into their head and called it a day."

The nonchalant way he says it makes my blood boil.

"Who?" Stress demands. "Who did you kill?"

He waves a hand through the air. "It doesn't matter. They're gone. Hell, I don't even think I can remember." Glancing at Freddie, he chuckles. "Do you?"

"Naw. Didn't really care enough to. I *do* know there were a few who decided to leave and I ended up killing 'em anyway." He smirks. "Figured they were the type who'd cause problems down the line. Decided to be proactive and take care of them before they became an issue."

As soon as the last word was out of Freddie's mouth, chaos erupts. I can't even make out who says what, there's so much yelling. Then it happened…

A gunshot. A grunt of pain.

Dodging to the side, I yank out my gun as I land on the ground behind the picnic table.

Angry shouts and sounds of running let me know everybody is ducking for cover. With only a few trees and some tables around us, that is hard to do. Glancing to my left, I spot Smoke on the ground, hand on his thigh, face scrunched up in pain, blood seeping between his fingers.

Lifting up slightly, I see Brash standing there, gun aimed at Smoke. I'm not even surprised he was the one who shot first.

More gunfire, several hitting the table I hid behind, one splintering the wood right by my face.

Bastards.

"Piece of shit!" I hear Smoke yell right before the *pop* of a gun. Glancing over, I see his gun in his right hand, slowly lowering back to the ground.

Whipping around, I see Brash on the ground, body crumpled, blood trickling out of a hole in his head, eyes staring sightlessly.

Movement to my left catches my attention. Fat Mike yanks his gun from his waistband, gaze locked on Smoke, who tries to pull himself behind cover.

I quickly scramble up, facing Fat Mike, gun pointed at his head. His eyes drill into mine, even as he keeps his gun pointed at Smoke.

"What are you going to do, Maverick?" he sneers. "Shoot me?"

I just stare at him, my gun steady.

"I bet you aren't even man enough to pull the trigger."

I stay silent. There are so many things I want to say to him. So much rage begging to be unleashed over what he's done to our club. But I realize none of that matters. Sweat trickles down the side of his face. The hand holding his gun wavers slightly. He's scared. Not sure why that makes me feel a mixture of happiness and sadness, but it does. Knowing he feels fear, even if for only a second, seems like justice for those he had killed.

"You just going to stand there all night? Weak and pathetic, as always. Well, I don't have time for this. You can just watch as I work my way through the group, saving your sorry ass for last. How does that sound?

"You all thought you were so smart, coming out here and confronting me. It's laughable. In the end, I'll fucking win. I always do, Maverick. You hear me, you sorry bastard?!"

His whole body shakes, spittle dripping out of the corner of his mouth. Yet the angrier he got, the calmer I became.

I open my mouth to reply, then stop, giving my head a mental shake. I refuse to allow him to drag me into an argument.

I don't remember squeezing the trigger. I feel the recoil, hear the crack of the bullet, see blood bloom on his chest over his heart.

Fat Mike crumples to the ground as I lower my gun. His mouth opens and closes as he gasps out his last few breaths, eyes wide open in shock as the life drains from them.

It's over.

Blowing out a breath I'm not aware I'm holding, I look around at the fight taking place around me.

I look to my left just as Fix shoots Skeeter and Freddie in quick succession, both men falling to the ground with bullet wounds in their heads. Blood trickles out of a cut in Fix's neck, yet seems fine otherwise.

I hear another shot or two ring out before everything goes quiet, eerie silence descending over the yard.

I walk up to Smoke and grip his arm, helping him stand, seeing the bullet had gone through his thigh. "I thought we agreed nobody was to get shot today," I joke.

"Funny," he grinds out, face contorting in pain.

The rest of our brothers join us, every one ribbing him as we slowly make our way inside, Smoke groaning with every step. I glance around the group as we walk. There are a few minor injuries, but we haven't lost a single one.

Thank fuck.

On the other hand, Fat Mike and every single one of his followers have been taken out. Even Poot, who'd obviously made his decision on which side he was on.

It really is a waste. But they made their choice. Now we have to live with the fallout.

Once we get Smoke back into the clubhouse, Talon and I help him sit on one of the barstools, while Viper grabs a clean rag to press onto his wound.

Fix and Dodger walk in with Cricket,

who looks like he'd taken a bullet to the shoulder. He growls at them to leave him alone, but they just roll their eyes and steer him toward one of the benches along the wall.

The guys give each other slaps on the back and fist bumps, laughing. I can feel how relieved everyone is.

"Question," Dodger yells over the talking. Everyone turns to him. "Actually, a couple.

"First, we don't have a club president or VP. How should we handle that?"

"Well..." I wrack by brain. Do our bylaws mention anything about how to handle something like this? I don't remember reading anything. "I think we should take the night, think over who we want for a president and VP. Tomorrow, we'll put it to a vote. Agreed?"

"Sounds good to me," Smoke says, hissing slightly as he shifts on the stool.

"Excellent." Dodger nods. "Next question. How can we convince Doc to come and look over our injuries?"

"Call him. If you explain what happened

and tell him everything has been taken care of, just like I promised, he'll come over."

He nods and turns to walk over to the end of the bar to use the phone.

"Fix." He looks at me. "Do you think you can take a few guys and get the yard cleaned up?"

"No problem." He looks around the room, nodding toward a few men. "We'll get it cleaned up in no time."

"Great."

Dodger walks back over and strides to Smoke's side. "Doc was a little hesitant at first, not that I blame him, but after I assured him he wouldn't have any trouble from anyone here, he agreed to come over."

Nodding, I glance around the room. Fix and a few guys have gone outside. But the ones who remained relaxed over a drink, the mood in the room seeming more tranquil than it has in months. I figure this is as good a time as any to sneak away, my thoughts turning to Jenny.

"I'm taking off, guys," I say, then look at Smoke. "You good?"

"Yeah, brother. You go on. We'll see you tomorrow for the meeting."

Nodding, I wave to everyone else and make my way outside. The minute I step out, I take a deep breath. It truly feels like a huge weight has been lifted off my shoulders.

Smiling, I swing a leg over my bike and head down the drive. It's time to see my girl.

Chapter 10
Jenny

"I'm here, Mama. Do you need any help with dinner?" I call out, setting my purse on the table by the front door.

When I was in my mid-twenties, I moved into a house not far from my parents. It wasn't much. Just a little two-bedroom. But it is mine. It's also nice being close to my parents. I love being around them, so I couldn't imagine moving far away.

My brother also has his own place. A townhouse close to downtown. He wanted to remain in the same town as his family and club. Just not that close. We liked to tease each other about it, but at the end of the day, we're still over at our parents' house more often than not.

Not that they complained, especially our dad. With how protective he's always been, I'm sure he would have preferred we never moved out at all. But I think us being close made him feel better when we left home.

Our mom, on the other hand, felt it was time for us to spread our wings and supported our decision when we each made up our minds to move out. Much to our father's frustration.

Tonight, just like most nights, I'm meeting my brother over at our parents' house. The only difference is my mind is on someone else.

Something is going on with Maverick. I can feel it. I don't know what, but I could hear the stress in his voice on the phone last night. Before we'd hung up, I made him promise to call me tonight. Every time my phone rings and it's not his number, my stomach drops.

With each hour that passes, the dread inside me continues to grow. My mind keeps playing out the worst-case scenarios, all of them ending in me never knowing what it would feel like to kiss him, touch him, have him hold me close.

"Hi, baby."

Glancing up, I smile as my mom walks out of the kitchen. "Hi, Mama." I give her a big hug, sighing at her familiar warmth. After a day of worrying, this is exactly what I need.

"Is that Jenny?"

I hear my dad's voice boom from the kitchen. Smiling, we walk in. My brother sits at the table, cold beer in front of him.

"Hey, sis," Mustang says, getting up to give me a hug.

"Hey." I hug him back, then walk over to where my dad leans against the counter, wrapping my arms around him. "What are we having tonight?"

"Your ma's making her fried chicken with mash potatoes."

"Oh, that sounds yummy." I turn to her. "Do you need me to do anything?"

"Nope. Everything's ready. Sit, sit. Here, babe. Please take the mashed potatoes over there with you."

I smile as my dad walks over and steals a kiss from my mom as he grabs the bowl. She laughs and swats at his arm playfully as he pulls away.

While we eat, the conversation flows. Sitting there quietly, smile on my face, I listen as my mom talks about the latest drama between one of the club members, Bet, and the *two* women he's been dating. How he desperately tried to keep them apart so they wouldn't find out about each other. Apparently, it all blew up the other day in the center of the clubhouse, Bet running for his life as the two women chased him out the door.

The conversation transitions into easier topics from there, like the new motorcycle parts Mustang got and my dad's recent cigar purchase. I try to get involved, but I just can't seem to pull myself out the funk I had slipped into.

As we finish up, I notice both my dad and brother occasionally checking their watches. I try to focus on what my mother is saying, something about the new shopping center in town, but my dad looks at his watch again, slight frown on his face.

"Is everything okay?" I ask, looking between my dad and brother.

"Yeah. Everything's fine. Just waiting on a phone call. Nothing to worry about," my dad assures me, giving me a smile before joining in on the conversation.

My brother gives me a small shrug, taking the last spoonful of mashed potatoes off his plate.

I wonder if the phone call has anything to do with Maverick. I don't push the issue because if this is club business, they won't talk about it anyway. Plus, my parents don't know Maverick and I have started talking, and I don't feel like getting into that conversation tonight.

As the evening goes on, I start to get anxious to get home, hoping Maverick will call soon and I can breathe again. It always takes me a good twenty minutes to leave, because saying goodbye in my family is always followed by at least one more conversation. Since I live so close and walked over earlier, my brother offers to drive me home, which I happily accept.

After giving him a quick hug, I hop out of his truck and make my way inside. The first thing I do is check my voicemail. Seeing no new messages, I sink down onto the couch and stare at the black screen of the tv. It's getting late. At least later than it usually is when Maverick calls. I don't know what to think about that.

Deciding sitting on the couch doesn't

make me feel better, I stand and make my way through the dark, quiet house. Taking a quick shower, I pull on a pair of sleep pants and an oversized DMC t-shirt. Trying not to stare at my phone sitting on the nightstand, I pick up the book I've been reading and open it up to where I'd left off, but even reading about a suave pirate doesn't stop my mind from wandering back to Maverick.

After reading the same paragraph for the third time, I sigh and toss it onto the floor next to the bed. Knowing sleep won't come easily, I reach for my television's remote to find something mindless to watch when I hear a light knock on my front door.

Frowning, I slide out of bed and make my way to the door, wondering who it could be.

It's not my family or members of the club because one, they wouldn't come by this late, and two, they all have a key. Besides a few friends from school and some people I work with, there is nobody else I can think of that would show up.

Getting to the door, I get up on my tiptoes to look through the peephole. I step back with a gasp, quickly unlock the door, and pull it open. The smile that spreads across my face matches the one I'm gazing at.

"Maverick," I whisper.

"Hi, Jenny. I hope you don't mind me stopping by. I know I should have called, but I... I really wanted to see you."

"I'm don't mind at all. I was actually just thinking about you." I hold out my hand.

"Really?" He takes my hand and steps towards me, moving me back into the house. "What were you thinking?"

"Honestly, I was worried. I've been hoping you'd call all day."

"Aw, baby. I'm fine. Actually, I'm more than fine. I'm great. Today was definitely stressful, but everything is good now."

"Yeah?"

"Yeah, and I wanted to come celebrate."

He closes and locks the door, never taking his eyes off mine. Placing his hands against my waist, he spins me and lifts me up, pressing my back against the cool wood of the door.

"And what are we celebrating?" I ask breathlessly, wrapping my legs around his waist.

"Our future," he moans, leaning in and running his nose along the side of my neck. I tilt my head to the side, encouraging him keep going. He trails kisses to the bend at my shoulder.

"Future," I pant, feeling a tingle shoot right to my core.

He pulls back. "Yes. I know we haven't known each other long, but I already feel like I need you in my life. Being with you, hearing your voice, having you in my arms, just feels right." He leans forward, taking my lips in a gentle kiss, stealing my breath. "Is it the same for you?"

Being with him not only feels right, but almost like fate. Like we were meant for each other.

"Yes," I gasp, pulling him back to me and kissing him deeply.

As our tongues tangle, I feel his erection pushing against my core.

I don't know how long we stay like that, enjoying the feeling of each other, kissing until we have to pull back to breathe, only to start back up again. I could stay in his arms forever, but the need to feel his skin against mine becomes undeniable, a chant in my mind that continues to grow.

Reaching behind his neck, I start to pull up his shirt. Smiling, he slides my feet back to the floor and takes a step back, yanking his shirt over his head. My mind stutters to a stop at the sight of his muscular abs, chest, arms. But what really catches my attention is a truly stunning tattoo of an eagle in flight. Its wingspan reaches from one shoulder to the other, its talons extended, gaze almost daring me to run.

While the eagle is impressive, each of his biceps also has extremely detailed tattoos. The right—a motorcycle, the club's name in bold letters under it. The left—a large anchor, an octopus curling almost protectively around it.

I've always been a sucker for tattoos. I lean forward and run my tongue over the top of one of the eagle's wings. I feel his muscles jump at the contact.

He places a hand on either side of my head, tilting it up so he can give me another kiss, this one deeper and more demanding.

I walk backward toward my bedroom. He pulls back from the kiss long enough to rip my shirt over my head, throwing it to the side. The heat in his gaze is almost enough to make me come right there. I moan as he reaches up to cup one of my breasts, pinching my nipple. He slams his lips against mine again, swallowing my gasp.

We stumble into my room, both of us trying to get the pants off the other as we fall onto the bed. Realizing his pants are stuck because of his boots makes me laugh.

"Shit," he chuckles, awkwardly rolling off me so he can pull off his boots and lose his pants. I wiggle out of my sleep pants, pulling myself toward my pillow. Watching him push his boxers down makes my mouth water. Reaching down, I push my finger into my opening, finding myself wet and ready. I can't stop the throaty moan, drawing his attention.

His heated gaze meets mine as he slowly climbs back onto the bed, eyes traveling over me as he lifts one of my legs, placing it over his shoulder.

"I can feel your warmth from here," he whispers. "I have to taste you. Can I?" he asks, leaning toward my core.

"Yes," I gasp.

His tongue snakes out, tasting me, then traveling over my clit. The sensations running through me make my whole body tingle. This man certainly knows what he's doing in the bedroom.

"Fuck, you're delicious," he says, his warm breath caressing me before placing his mouth over my core once again, sucking lightly, sending shock wave after shock wave through my entire body. I grab his head with both hands as I rock my hips, demanding more.

"I can't... I need..." My voice sounds breathy as I try to explain what my body's craving.

He pulls back to give me a sinful smile, his lips and chin damp. "I know what my baby needs." Gripping my hips, he kneels between my thighs, lifting my hips up, opening me father.

I grip the sheets as he sucks my clit, then dips his tongue into my wetness. He repeats this action, driving me crazy, not knowing how much longer I can hold on, my moans getting louder.

"That's it," he growls, pushing one, then two fingers into me while continuing to suck on my clit.

My orgasm hits me suddenly as I scream out, back lifting off the bed. He continues to pump his fingers into me, prolonging my orgasm for what feels like minutes, leaving me gasping.

I open my eyes when he pulls back and reaches into his pants pocket, pulling out a condom. He rips it open and rolls it onto his impressive erection, making me moan. Tearing my eyes from it, I meet his deep blue eyes.

"You're mine," he growls, crawling on top of me. I feel the tip of his dick against my entrance. Whimpering, I wrap my legs around him, urging him into me. "Say it," he demands.

"Yes," I moan as he pushes in just a little before pulling back out.

"Yes what?" He thrusts into me.

"I'm yours!" I scream. I don't remember ever feeling so full. As he sets a punishing pace, I know nobody could ever make me feel like this. Only Maverick.

"God, you feel so good. Your pussy grips my dick like it can't get enough."

His words push me toward another orgasm. The sounds of skin smacking against skin and our panting fill the room, getting louder and louder as he picks up his pace.

"Yes," he growls, leaning down. His hot breath sears my ears and neck as our sweat-covered bodies rub against each other. "I want to feel you come around my dick."

"I'm so close," I moan, grasping the back of his neck.

He shifts his hips, changing the angle just enough that his next thrust pushes me over the edge. I scream Maverick's name as he chases his own release.

"That's it," he growls. "Fuck yeah, Jenny." Pulling out, he slams into me one more time and stills, moaning loudly.

This feeling is intoxicating. I want to experience it over and over again. Honestly, I don't think I'll ever get enough of this man.

As he starts to relax, his breathing ragged, he pulls back. He stares into my eyes for a heartbeat before giving me a breathtaking smile.

"Hi," he whispers.

"Hi," I murmur back with a smile. Reaching up, I run my hands through his deliciously disheveled hair. I pull him toward me, gently touching his lips with mine, moaning softly against his mouth.

He pulls away and slips out of me, my body complaining about the loss of contact. "We should get cleaned up."

"We should," I agree, chuckling when we don't move. "I'm not sure I can get up yet."

"Me, either," he chuckles, taking a couple deep breaths before pushing himself up. Maverick gently lifts my legs off him and moves away, sliding from the bed and walking toward my bathroom.

I watch him walk back out, rubbing a

towel over his chest and abs. He makes his way over to me, leaning down and gently moving the towel over my skin, leaving me feeling cared for in a way no other lover ever has. Dropping the towel to the floor, Maverick crawls back into bed, lying next to me, softly playing with my hair.

"Are you staying?" I ask gently.

His gaze searches mine. "Do you want me to?"

Staring into his eyes, I suddenly can't imagine not having him here. Which is crazy. This is all happening so quickly. I should quietly back away, slow things down.

But I can't.

The thought of not learning all I can about this man, of never feeling his presence, of not knowing what it feels like to be cared for by him is not something I want to consider.

So I tell him the only thing I can. Yes, I want him around. Want him to stay. Tonight. Maybe the next. And the next after that.

He kisses me. A long kiss full of promises and love.

When he asks me how long I want him to stay, I give him the only answer I can.

"Forever, Maverick. I want you forever."

Epilogue
Maverick

26 years later

Walking out of my office, I smile, laughter filtering into the hallway from the bar. It has taken a long time to get here, and I'm still sometimes surprised with how far we've come.

The day after that fateful night, we took a vote on who should be president and VP. Much to my surprise, as well as Smoke's, I was to be president with him as VP.

Saying I was humbled was putting it mildly. I vowed to them to never do anything to make them regret voting that way, telling them I'd strive to take care of this club and their families each and every day.

Another surprise that following morning was learning Poot had survived. We doctored him back to health, then sent him on his way. It had been a gamble, letting him leave the club like that, but it turned out to be the right choice.

We didn't have another brother's blood on our hands. Last I heard, he'd found his place down in LA.

Cleaning up Fat Mike's mess had been a task. The main issue had been severing any connection with Tick and his Jackals. That took almost three years, but once we got them to realize we were more trouble than we were worth, things moved pretty smoothly.

And now, over two decades later, I can say the Wicked Rogues are once again whole, healthy, and back to being the club it had been when I'd joined...if not better.

Sure, there were some other issues along the way, but nothing we couldn't handle. We also had a lot of great times over the years. Brothers who had left came back as soon as they heard the news, like Dog, who'd barely escaped Freddie one night.

On a more personal note, I took Jenny's desire to keep me forever and made it reality, much to her father's and brother's dismay. I think Mustang was opposed to us being together because he didn't think anybody was good enough for his sister, but both men warmed up to me after a while... A *long* while.

I know Brick respected me, just as I respected him, but he was adamant he didn't want this life for his daughter. I couldn't blame the man for that, so I made sure to prove to him every chance I got that I would take care of Jenny. Her mother, on the other hand, told me that if her daughter was happy, she was happy. However, she made sure to tell me her husband wasn't the only one who could make people "disappear". The hard look in her eyes made me stifle my laughter, because I knew she was serious. But hearing her sweet mother tell me that made me realize I was going to love being a part of this family. Which was good, since I planned on being around a long time.

So, one year to the day of our first night together, I proposed.

I'm not a huge romantic, but I've been told I have my moments. That day, I took Jenny for a ride, drove to the beach, and proposed as the sun set over the water. She cried, then gave me one of her heart-stopping smiles as she said "yes".

That one word had changed my world,

making me wonder how I had ever lived without her.

We set the date for two weeks in the back yard of the clubhouse. We'd partied through the night, then Jenny and I took off for a week in Tahoe. Having her all to myself, laughing with me throughout the day as we enjoyed the sites, then moaning with me at night, was perfect.

Nine months later, Cole was born.

I didn't think I could love anyone as much as I loved Jenny. The day Cole came into this world and I held him in my arms for the first time, my whole world changed once again.

He was rambunctious, adorable, and the perfect mixture of both myself and Jenny, growing from a delightful toddler to an amazing man. I couldn't be prouder.

Then, seven years after Cole was born, I received a call I'd been dreading over the years. One I knew was inevitable. My sister, who had disappeared all those years earlier, had lost her life to the drugs she loved more than herself. I had no time to think too hard on the *what if's* because, to my surprise, I learned I had a niece.

One who needed me, needed her family. So, with the full support of Jenny, Cole, and the club, I took off as fast as I could.

Abigail...

As she got into the truck after I picked her up from the police station, her soft voice informed me she preferred Abby. It was both adorable and heartbreaking.

I wish I had known about her sooner. Been able to shield her from the horrors no child should witness.

I can't change the past, but I've sure spent every day since making up for it. We all have, and we all love her dearly.

Walking into the bar area, I spot her and Cole shooting pool with Cross, Abby giving both men a hard time. Cole is prospecting for the club and will probably be a member soon. He has worked hard and has found his way in this life, just like I knew he would. Of course, Jenny and I were worried about him and Abby growing up around the club, but decided that it was far safer for them here. Better for them to know the dangers and how to take care of themselves.

Abby looks up from lining up her shot and waves at me, smiling. Then she goes back to the game, shooting. Right into the left pocket.

"You heading out?"

Hearing the rough voice behind me, I turn to see Smoke.

"Yeah. Thought I'd head down to Brimmer's for a drink before heading home. I'm making meatloaf tonight. You gonna swing by?"

"Yeah. I have a few phone calls to make, then I was going to head out myself."

Knowing he was going to call his brothers, I nod. They had gone to our New Orleans' charter to help the president, King, with some territory problems. When he'd called in need of assistance, I knew the triplets were the best ones to send.

"How are the boys doing?"

"Good. They almost have King's issues handled, but I think they plan on sticking around for a while once they're done. Unless we need them, of course."

"Tell them to enjoy a little downtime. They deserve it."

"Will do." He nods, turning toward the hallway. "I'll see you in a bit."

Waving a hand over my head, I make my way out to my bike, only stopping briefly to talk with a few brothers. Before too long, I'm on the road, weaving my way along the street.

Pulling into Brimmer's parking lot, I notice it is fairly empty for this time of day. That suits me fine, though. I just want to have a quick drink before heading home.

Nodding to a few patrons as I enter, I walk over to the bar and take a seat, sighing. Signaling to the bartender, Tim, I request a glass of whatever they have on tap. He's been working here for the last few years and always makes sure to ask about the family. He sets the glass in front of me. We chat for a bit before he has to take care of other patrons.

I glance around the dimly lit bar, rock music coming from the small speakers in the walls. Almost of its own accord, my foot starts tapping out the beat on the bottom of the bar. Smiling at how relaxed I feel, I take a sip from my glass and slowly scan the room.

It isn't too long before I spot a stranger sitting at the end of the bar.

Now, I don't know everyone in town. But I feel comfortable in saying I know almost all the regulars that frequent Brimmers. Newcomers tend to stick out.

When Tim walks up to give me another beer, I nod in the man's direction. "What's his deal?"

"Not sure. He hasn't said much. Been sitting there quietly for the last hour or so, only asking for a beer and some pretzels."

Humming, I nod as Tim walks away.

I'm a sucker for someone in need. Always have been. Jenny will say I'm a magnet for strays. Hell, half the guys I've brought into the club since I became president were down on their luck, looking for a place to belong.

And I gave them just that. Stability. A family.

This man definitely looks like he needs help. Shoulders hunched, head down, face drawn... He looks like he's on the verge of giving up.

Grabbing my half-empty glass, I walk toward the man. Sitting on the barstool beside him, I wait until he glances my way before saying anything.

I start the conversation simply. How great the beer selection is, how the restaurant down the street serves the best burgers, and if he ever needs any work done on his car or truck, there's no place better to go than Jack's.

I can tell he's a little annoyed by my presence. That slowly melts away as I begin talking about personal things. Jenny, my kids, some of the antics the boys in the club have gotten into. After a while, I get him talking, answering some questions. He doesn't go into detail, but it's a start.

As I finish my beer, I stand, glancing around the bar before looking back at the man. His steel blue eyes still look a little guarded, yet meet mine without flinching.

"You planning on being in town for a while?" I ask.

He shrugs, glancing down at his beer before looking back at me. "Probably a day or two."

"Wanna meet up tomorrow? I could take you around, introduce you to some people. You know, just in case you decide to stick around longer."

He seems unsure. I can practically see him calculating the pros and cons. Just when I think he's going to decline, he nods sharply. "Yeah, sure. It might be cool to meet some people."

"Then I'll meet you here tomorrow around two. Sound good?"

"Works for me."

"Good." I hold out my hand. "Name's Maverick."

"Tristan," he responds, shaking my hand. "Tristan Knight."

"Well, Knight, it's nice meeting you. See you tomorrow."

"Yeah. See you then."

As I leave, I glance back and see him

sitting there, staring at his beer, body relaxing slightly. He's in trouble, and whatever the trouble is has him spooked.

Sometimes a person just needs a lifeline. Someone to give them an option to take another path.

I don't know if I'll be able to help him. Hell, I'm not even sure he's ready to accept help. He's so damn guarded, having built a concrete wall around himself.

But he's agreed to meet up, and that's a start.

It'll be up to him if he wants to stick around, wants to stop running from whatever is chasing him. A lot of the guys in the club were running from one thing or another, each bringing their own problems.

He may be in trouble, may be getting dogged by something that could rear its ugly head at any point, but it's not something any of us would shy away from.

Getting on my bike and heading home, I smile, looking forward to having Jenny in my arms.

E.F. Rose

This life is tough, but I wouldn't trade it for the world.

I have a beautiful, strong wife, two amazing kids, and am the president of the Wicked Rogues MC.

What could be better than that?

120 | P a g e

Turn the page to read the first chapter from book one of the Wicked Rogues series....

Forever Knight

E.F. Rose

Chapter 1
Knight

January 22, 2016
FBI Headquarters
San Francisco, California

"I'm sorry, Tristan. There's nothing else I can do."

Sitting there, I can only shake my head. How can he lie to me like that? Tell me there isn't anything else he can do when we both knew that's not true. Frank and I have been close since I was sworn in. Shit, he was the one who found me. Brought me into the Bureau. He's the father I never had. A mentor as I fought to make my way through the bullshit that came with being a Fed.

I've always backed him, too. Pulled his ass out of more messes than I can remember.

Yet now, when I need him the most, when I feel like I'm drowning in my fucking pain, he gives me this line of shit?

My blood begins to boil as I stare across the desk at him.

People keep telling me it's understandable to be so angry, considering all that has transpired. I thought that was it, too. I was just angry, hurt. But *angry* doesn't seem quite adequate. I feel a deep rage, which grows with each lie leaving Frank's lips. Hell, it takes all my restraint to not reach for my gun right now.

A sneer forms on my lips as I glare at him, fake sympathy on his face. If I have to hear the "I'm so sorry" and "everything will be all right" bullshit one more time, I am going to fucking lose it!

Everything is *not* going to be all right. How can it be?

My sister, my confidant, the only family I had left, had been murdered. No, not just murdered. Butchered by a madman! Images of Jess' mutilated body flash through my mind.

But the worst part?

I was the one who found her.

Jess had called several times that night, but I was on a case, my phone on silent. It wasn't until leaving the office the next afternoon that I had been able to check my messages. Her frantic pleas clearing the exhaustion from my brain, I ran to my car and threw it into drive, tires squealing, the fear in her voice tearing at me. Among her hysterical cries, I could pick out details. Someone was in the house, holding her captive, and insisted she call me, and only me. Message after message, I heard the tone in Jess' voice growing more hopeless.

I don't really remember the drive, only the blur of cars I passed. What I do recall is my stomach churning, hands clenching the steering wheel.

Mere blocks from her house, I pushed the button on my steering wheel to replay the latest message on my phone. Jess' voice wobbled through the speakers, making my hands grip the wheel even tighter.

"Tristan... Why aren't you answering? Oh god. He said he's tired of waiting for you. That he needs to move on with his plans. What does he mean?" Her voice cracked as she sobbed loudly. *"Why is he doing this? Tris–"*

A shuffling sound came through. I could still hear her uncontrolled sobs as a man's gravelly voice rumbled through the car, catching me so off guard, I swerved.

"Agent Marcs... Tristan," he said with a tisk. *"You should have answered your phone. Now this pretty little flower and I are going to have to party without you. Maybe it's better this way. After all... How's that saying go?*

Two's a party, three's a crowd? But I don't want you to worry, Tristan..." He chuckled. Jess' sobs of despair caused a cold sweat to break out on my skin. *"I'll take good care of her."*

With that, the line went dead.

Screeching to a stop in front of the house, I scrambled out of the car and drew my weapon, never even stopping to think I should probably call for backup.

Even now, a year and four months later, the whole scene plays out in my mind like a silent movie. One that repeats relentlessly in my every waking moment and through my dreams.

The front door was slightly open. The air inside had been stale, the metallic smell of blood assaulting my nose as I cautiously made my way through the first floor of her two-story house. Jess' gorgeous house, so neat and tidy, our family photos covering the walls.

My mind latched on to the realization that she would never again laugh at our silly picture from Great America, or eat her Chinese takeout on the floor by the coffee table.

Once I walked into the dining room, only one thing encompassed my vision.

The blood...

So much fucking blood.

It ran down the walls, thick and dark, pooling on the floor near the dining room table. Denial spread through me as I stared at it. Our mother's white tablecloth was now a reddish brown, and in the center lay Jess. Or what was left of her.

I vaguely remember walking to the table and staring into her vacant eyes, the only part of her untouched.

That was where the cops found me. My roars of pure rage had startled the neighbors, causing them to run to their phones. At least that was what I was told.

One year and four months since I had lost my baby sister.

One year, four months, three weeks since we had lowered her into the ground on that cold, October day.

A blanket of dead leaves had covered the ground, my boots crunching loudly as I moved up to her closed casket, placing my hand on the lid. I hadn't cried since I'd found her. All my emotions combined into a single need to find the bastard who had done this to her. There was no room for tears in my need for revenge.

There were over a hundred people at the funeral that day. Some I knew, many I didn't. Agents, local PD, teachers from the district Jess worked for, even some guys we grew up with. Everyone professed how sorry they were for what had happened, while silently being glad it hadn't happened to one of their sisters.

Robotically, I repeated my thanks, shaking hands and receiving hugs, all the while seething with my need to find Jess' killer. It wasn't really until that moment, though, silently standing there as her casket was lowered into the ground, that I made my vow. My fellow agents, many of whom I had known since the academy, all stated their willingness to help, stand by me to find the bastard who had taken my sister from me.

Unfortunately, I later found out those promises were as hollow as the apologies that followed.

At the time, though, I had trusted them, blindly accepting their false support.

Even with very little evidence left at the crime scene, I'd located the killer within months. *Months*! Ted Steele, nicknamed the *Butcher of the Bay* by the local papers. He'd been taken in without a fight, smiling the whole way. I'd grinned right back. The smug bastard could smile all he wanted. He'd be behind bars soon enough, then quickly moved to death row.

It was an open-and-shut case.

It had taken a little over a year to schedule a court date. We needed everything to be done right. No loose ends. We had done everything we could to guarantee a conviction.

Or so I had thought.

It took less than a week in court for me to realize I'd been wrong.

The defense brought up some claims that evidence was mishandled, possibly planted. Which I knew was bullshit, because I personally made sure everything was collected, cataloged, and tagged properly. But the judge just nodded, stating he felt the defense had a valid argument, and threw the case out. Every last fucking piece of evidence... Gone with a slam of his gavel, giving Steele his freedom.

That was two weeks ago. The shock of watching my sister's killer wink at me as he got into his SUV had finally worn off. Now here I am, sitting in Frank's office, listening to his fake concern. I ball my hands into fists as I glare at him.

"Tristan? Have you heard anything I've said?" Frank asks, placing his elbows on his desk and leaning forward.

"Yeah, Frank," I sneer. "It's the same

shit you've been repeating since the judge *claimed* we messed up on the fucking evidence!"

"Now, Tristan—"

"I *know* that evidence was bagged and tagged correctly." Gritting my teeth, I mimic Frank's posture by leaning over the desk. "I oversaw it myself! Nothing was mishandled. I don't know what that judge was looking at, but it wasn't what we collected."

"Tristan," Frank huffs, frustration clear on his face. "We've gone over this. I know you're upset—"

"*Upset*?! That's putting it pretty fucking mildly, don't you think?"

"*But...*," he continues, as if I hadn't interrupted, "sometimes things just happen. We'll get Ted Steele for something else. Don't think he's going to just get away next time."

Clenching my jaw, I growl, "Next time? Are you fucking shitting me?! He's gone, Frank! Walked out those courtroom doors a free man. There's no way we're going to get him on anything again, and you know it. Shit, *he* fucking knows it! The smirk on that bastard's face as he left that day said as much."

The walls of his office feel like they're

closing in. The monster who had chopped up my beautiful baby sister is out there, free to do it again. It shouldn't have happened. I'd repeatedly gone over the events in my head, and everything had been done by the book. So how in the hell was the defense able to convince the judge otherwise? There's no way! Unless...

I feel my mind spin as it lands on the only conclusion that makes sense.

Standing abruptly, my chair topples over and hits the floor with a bang. "Someone on the inside had to be helping him."

Frank's eyes twitch slightly before they widen in disbelief. "You can't be serious."

"It's the only thing that makes any sense, Frank. Don't you think it's funny that an air-tight case gets thrown out by some bullshit claims?"

"And who do you think this phantom insider is?" Frank asks slowly.

I throw up my hands. "Who fucking knows? It could be the defense lawyer...or a member of the PD...or... Shit. Maybe it's the fucking judge himself! Maybe it's all three. For all I know, the judge was bought and paid for by the shithead's lawyer."

"Tristan, I think you're reaching." Frank shakes his head. "Listen, even if...and that's a *big* if...the judge were paid off, how much do you think it would cost to make something like that happen? I mean, it's not like Ted Steele's a rich man. I don't think he could afford the kind of cash it would take to pull off something like that. Not to mention Judge McGowen is a good man. He's heard multiple cases and has always, *always* done the right thing."

"Yeah, but—"

"No, Tristan. I get you're upset...hell, who wouldn't be?...but to accuse a judge of being dirty... That's going too far. Shit, if what you just said came out, it could ruin your career. I really think you need to let this one go."

I stare at him, aghast. "How can you ask me to do that? Did you see what he did to Jess? To my *baby sister*?" I shake my head vehemently. "I can't just let this go, Frank. I will get to the bottom of it. There's something rotten going on here, and I'm going to do everything I can to discover what it is."

He blinks, then takes a deep breath, blowing it out. "Well, unfortunately, it's not up to you to look into anything. At least not anymore. I'm putting you on leave—"

"You can't—"

"I *can*, and I am!" Frank states, standing. He holds out his hand, steely gaze never leaving mine. "Give me your gun and your badge."

I narrow my eyes. Of all the endings to this meeting I had imagined, this was not one of them. Clenching my fists, I try to slow my breathing, to no avail. Chest tightening, I pull my badge from my pocket and flip it open, looking down at the shiny, gold metal, remembering the day I received it. I was so happy, the moment made better by the pride on Jess' face.

"Mom would be so proud of you," she whispered, hugging me tightly. "I know she's looking down on us right now, smiling at how well we are both doing."

Resting my chin on her head, I closed my eyes. "I hope so."

"I know so, Tris." Pulling back, she met my gaze. "I know she is, just as I am. After taking care of me for so many years, I'm happy to see you do this for yourself. You deserve it."

"I love you, sis."

"I love you, too, brother. To the moon and back."

Her words echo through my head as I

run my thumb over the cool metal. How has my life come to this?

If I were being honest with myself, I really don't feel the same about my job anymore. So much has changed since Jess was taken from me. I feel my connection with the FBI, my pride in the badge, fading a little more every day.

Looking up at Frank, I pull my gun from its holster. I grasp them both briefly before slapping them into his palm. "I don't think this job is for me anymore, Frank."

"Well, I'm sorry to hear that," he says evenly, completely unaffected. I may as well have told him what I wanted for lunch.

Keeping myself from reacting to his callous response, I gave him a curt nod. "I'll have my resignation letter on your desk by morning."

"Don't worry about coming in, Tristan. I know things have been...overwhelming for you lately. A simple email will suffice. It was a pleasure working with you." He pulls out his top drawer, unceremoniously dropping my badge and gun into it.

I stand there a moment longer, watching him sit and begin to type away on his keyboard, not looking at me again, before turning and walking out the door. Taking a few steps down the hall, I stop and lean against the wall. After all this time, I can't believe he would just dismiss me like that. Discarded like yesterday's trash.

Everything I want to say to him, to all my so-called friends within the agency, rush through my mind. Why the hell am I holding back? I'm quitting anyway.

I turn back to Frank's office and step up to the door, stopping at the sound of his low, even voice.

"No, I don't think he's going to be a problem."

Curiosity piqued, I glance around. Seeing nobody, I step closer to the door and lean toward it, hearing Frank's chair scratch against the hardwood floor.

"Of course he had questions... I know... I told him to take leave, but he decided to resign... Yeah... That's what I'm saying."

My eyes narrow. Who in the hell is he talking to? And why does he think I'll be a problem?

Images of what went down in the courtroom flash in my mind. Everyone staying so calm when the judge threw out the case.

"I understand... He should be home tonight... No. He should be alone."

Frank's words send chills down my spine as I slowly back away from the door. Turning, I quickly make my way to the stairs, taking two at a time as I rush down the four flights to the garage.

Whoever Frank had been talking to obviously had a hand in acquitting Ted Steele. Hell, it could have even been the man himself. Add in the fact Frank was obviously dirty and, well... I'll have to dissect that little tidbit later.

Striding across the garage, I stop next to my Honda Civic. I take a step back, looking at it for a second. If I were gunning for someone, I would damn sure know what kind of car they drove.

I open the driver's side door and lean in. After retrieving my personal gun from the glove compartment, slipping it into the back waistband of my pants, and the cash I hid in the side compartment, I pull my wallet from my back pocket.

If all the cases I'd worked for the Bureau had taught me one thing it was how to disappear. Grabbing my driver's license, credit cards, and medical information, I toss each onto the seat with a sigh. Then I pull out a picture of Jess and me, smiling slightly.

It was taken in Monterey several years ago. She loved the beach, insisting we spend time there whenever we could. She said it was good for the soul, and with my line of work, I occasionally needed the calm of the ocean.

Sliding the picture into my wallet, I grip the cool leather tightly for a few moments before sliding it into my back pocket. With a final sigh, I drop my keys onto the seat and close the car door.

The gun feels heavy against my back as I jog through the garage. Stepping out into the bright San Francisco sun, I glance around at the busy street. People walk by as they enjoy the beautiful day. Making sure my shirt hides my gun, I step into the crowd, trying to blend in. Weaving around people, I begin to plan. To decide where to go next. I'll definitely have to change my last name. I've been at my job too long, dealt with too many criminals, to keep it. Luckily, my first name isn't as widely known. I need to figure this all out, and quickly.

One thing I did know for certain. One way or another, I was going to find Ted Steele...and fucking kill him.

Forever Knight is available at amazon.com

Thank You

Thank you so much for reading Maverick Rising. I truly hope you all enjoyed reading about Maverick's rise in the club and his growing connection with Jenny. Their story will continue on throughout the series and I look forward to sharing more about this amazing couple with you.

I'd like to thank my family and friends for all their support. Your input and support is truly appreciated.

I'd also like to thank all of the amazing members in my FB group, The Official E.F. Rose Fan Group, for your continued support and ability to always make me smile. You guys are the best and I'm thankful for your friendship every day.

Also, a huge thank you to my editor, who always knows how to make my novels shine. I know this story wouldn't be as great as it is without her help.

Until next time, be sure to love hard, stay safe, and always be true to yourself!

Love,

E.F. Rose

P.S. If you enjoyed Maverick and Jenny's story, please stop by and leave a review. Your words help bring my characters to more people and, in turn, help me to continue giving them life. Thank you again! Xx

About the Author

E.F. Rose and family have found their corner of the world in the Central Valley of California. She has always enjoyed writing and considers herself to be a multi-genre author, with urban fantasy and dark romance being her main focus. If she isn't writing up a storm, she can be found chatting with friends, reading a good book, or spending time with her husband and son.

If you would like to know more about E.F. Rose and her work, you can find all her social media and book links at https://linktr.ee/E_F_Rose, or you can reach out to her at emilyfrose13@gmail.com.

"You are my drive, my inspiration, the life behind my words."

More Work From E.F. Rose

Echoes (A Book of Poetry – 2nd Edition)

The Fallen Guardians Series

Divinely Entwined (Book 1) – Christian & Ella

Bound in Fate (Book 2) – Manuel & Hayley

Tangled in Tinsel (Book 2.5)

Faithfully Entangled (Book 3) - Nicholas & Amy

Twisted Mercy (Book 4) – Cyrus' Story *coming soon*

Wicked Rogues

Maverick Rising (Prequel) – Maverick & Jenny

Forever Knight (Book 1) – Tristan & Abby

Always Abby (Book 2) – Tristan & Abby
coming soon

Standalone Novellas

Colin's Valentine's Day Surprise – Colin & Brett

An Angel for Christmas – Shane & Dax